STIKINE
By
Rosalyn Stowell

The Ten Commandments
(Not the Ten Suggestions)
Thou shalt not have any other Gods
before Me
Thou shalt not make unto thee any graven
images
Thou shalt not take the name of The Lord
thy God in vain
Remember the Sabbath Day and keep it
Holy
Honor thy Father and thy Mother
Thou shalt not commit murder
Thou shalt not commit adultery
Thou shalt not steal
Thou shalt not bear false witness against
thy neighbor
Thou shalt not covet

Books by Rosalyn Stowell
Don't Use A Chainsaw In The Kitchen (cookbook)
Trilogy: PAW Novels (Post Apocalyptic World)*
The Beginning - Book 1*
The Dark Of Night - Book 2*
The Dawn - Book 3*
Alaskan Gold - Romance Novel
Alaskan Alibi - Suspense
The Alaskan Mosquito Cookbook (Humor)
My Alaskan Sketch Book (artwork)
Stikine - Suspence

Chapter 1

What an awful odor and her head is feeling like it has been used as a punching bag. Oh, that's right, when George came home last night, he did take a swing at her and that was the last thing she remembered until the smell woke her up a few moments ago.

She starts to get up but realizes she is tied firmly to the bed frame she is laying on. Now that is just the last straw. If George thinks he can get away with treating her like this, he has another think a'coming.

She tries to open her eyes but feels there is something across her face that she can't move away from. So she methodically starts trying to work her hands free and to rub her face back and forth to move whatever is across her eyes.

As she works, her hands become more loosely bound but not quite enough to pull free when she realizes she is hearing the sound of a motor slowly drawing nearer. She works faster on her hands and finally slips one free just as the motor shuts off.

The sound of footsteps coming nearer, makes her decide to pretend to still be tied and unconscious so she slides her hand back into the loops behind her back and lays still.

A door is pushed open across the space from her and someone says it looks like the woman is still out. Someone else mutters it will probably be better that way, just leave her and she won't know anything. Some more mutters and the door is shut again.

She quickly pulls her hand out again and reaches for her face. There is a cloth tied around her eyes so she just pushes an edge up high enough to look out under without removing it entirely. She looks around the area she is in and it looks like one of the old cannery shacks near the beach where they used to process fish many years ago. This is miles from her home and no roads out here, only boat access.

She quickly checks and she is still wearing the clothes she walked in the door after work in, just before George hit her. Since there is no heat in this building and it is never all that hot most of the time in Southeast Alaska, she is glad she still has her coat on, even if it is summer.

She carefully removes the ties around her ankles and sits on the edge of the bed frame a few minutes, trying to get her body responding correctly again. There has been no sound of a motor leaving and she doesn't know where the men are, so it might be best to just play passed out all the time they are here, unless she can see a clear means of escape. She didn't recognize the voices, but then, she wasn't allowed out except to work, and there were no men working there. So she really didn't know many people around here.

George was so insecure that he kept her practically under lock and key, so she was used to having to escape from different situations. He would go through spells of allowing her some freedom, but if anyone stopped to talk to her or asked him how she was doing, he was positive they were messing around with her and then back to being locked up again.

She had loved him once, but his actions certainly didn't nurture love or allow it to grow. Now she felt a growing contempt for his continued adolescent behavior and punching her out last night, if it was last night, was the final straw.

She slowly and carefully starts walking around the small room she is in, looking for some way to see outside and maybe be able to tell if the men were close or somewhere farther away.

Partway around the wall, she stumbles over something on the floor and finds George. The room is so dark, she doesn't realize just what it is, until she stoops down and feels a face, then the familiar whiskers and overweight body. She smothers back a scream as it finally dawns on her that he is probably dead.

She drags him carefully back toward the bed and after many tries, manages to get him up on it in her place and ties the cloth around his face like it was around hers. Anyone just looking in quickly might think it was her, if she gained a hundred pounds and grew whiskers, but she was hoping they just glanced in and left.

She hears voices again, coming toward the shed and she moves over behind the door, picking up a piece of metal that must have been a part of a boat frame at one time. It is solid and at least makes her feel a bit better to hold it in her hands while her knees are shaking.

The door starts to open and someone calls from farther down the beach. The person opening the door just glances in and sees a shape on the bed and closes the door. There is the sharp odor of gasoline and the whoosh of fire as he walks away.

The motor starts back up and revs, then fades away and she now has to find a fast way out of this flimsy shed. The door is already leaking in smoke and too hot to touch. The window is boarded over, but fear adds strength and she manages to pull the frame loose and push the plywood off the window.

She looks around quickly to see if anything is handy that she could use, runs back over to

check on George and yes, he is really dead.
She pats his pockets and grabs the lighter and
knife. His hat and heavy coat are on the floor
so she grabs them as she goes by, and
manages to only slightly scrape away some
skin as she goes out the window. The smell
outside is terrible and she finds sign of an
illegal fish trap having been run from the old
site.

There is still a fresh fish on the cleaning
table and she grabs it as she goes by. Fish is
not a favorite meal, but it might be her only
meal for quite a while. This camp is a long
way from the end of the road and that is a
long way from town, for someone walking.

None of the towns around here are
attached to a road system, just the short
stretches of road that people live along that
go a ways beside the beaches.
The only way to travel is boat or airplane, so
most families have boats here. She and
George were not one of them.

There is a broken handled shovel leaning
against the side of the burning shed, so she
takes that, too. A bit farther out and she finds
a torn burlap bag that has been discarded, so
she stuffs the fish into the bag and ties
George's coat around her waist, the hat on
her head and she now has almost too much to
carry as it is bulky, not heavy.

She moves into the heavy trees and puts her

load down so she can check and see if there is anything else handy that she might be able to use, on her trek back to town.

So far, she has not seen anyone but she is not sure where they have gone and if they are coming back. Having set the fire, they must not be intending to use this site again. But she can't be sure, so she inches along, trying to see everywhere at once.

The shed is fully engulfed in flames so she says a brief prayer for George. She might not still love him, but anyone deserves a better end than that.

She inches along, trying to blend in and become part of the scenery. She finds a fillet knife someone has dropped and a discarded pack with a broken strap. She drags it behind her as she scoots along, trying to find every little thing anyone may have dropped or thrown away. When she finds the can dump, she quickly grabs a large juice can and a couple of the empty stew cans. They can be used to cook in. Some pieces of wire will have many uses, so she grabs it, also. She might try to dig down through the pile and see what else she can find, but she hears a boat motor again, and grabs her supplies and fades back into the trees.

Southeast Alaska is the perfect place to hide, all that has to be done is hold still under some brush and there is always some brush.

Just as long as no Devils Club is in the way, everything is okay.

From her spot under the brush, she watches a boat pull up to the makeshift dock. The two men in it are arguing and one is sounding extremely angry.
When he sees the smoldering remains of the shed, he gets even angrier. The shed has collapsed and is a mound of burning lumber and some timbers from the roof. The rusty tin roof is twisted and practically glowing.

One man is shouting about the woman was supposed to be left alive and turned loose, she would be the perfect one to pin her husband's death on, since they had stupidly killed him. But he was not supposed to be killed. People turning up dead tended to bring investigators. Everyone in town knew he didn't treat her well. Look what condition she was in when they brought her out here. Some of the people in town would probably have given her a medal for getting rid of him. Thirty years ago, she wouldn't even have been arrested for it. Kill an illegal fish and go to jail, kill a mean husband and they helped plan a party, practically. Women were not plentiful in town.

Now, she would possibly get arrested, but they probably would let her go after listening to folks around town. He called the other man all kinds of names and the other man was slowly getting really angry. The more man #1 kept on, the more man #2 was almost steaming.

When he reached into the boat for the fishing spear, she almost yelled out a warning, but was afraid she would be next. Guy #1 must have heard something because he turned around just as the other man shot the spear and it almost missed him. His shot from his pistol didn't miss man #2.

The spear was still sticking out of his side where it had creased along his ribs but caught in the coat fabric and didn't do as much damage as it could have.

The wounded man stumbled a bit getting back into the boat, but he managed to get it turned and headed away again. She stayed crouched a bit longer then walked back to the can pile to see if she could quickly find anything else of use before starting her long walk back to the end of the road, if she could manage to get that far.

Anya found a couple of bottles with lids and she could rinse them out to carry water in. Even though Southeastern Alaska is a rain forest, it is hard to find clear drinking water.

A lot of the water looks like brewed tea and is colored from running through rotten vegetation among other things. It is usually foamy around the edges also and not the best flavored drink in the world. Any clear fresh water is to be treasured and carried along as much as possible. Of course there is always the ocean nearby.

It looks so tranquil and can be mirror smooth as no waves or breakers roll in past the outer islands. It is like living beside a large lake that fluctuates in levels with the water rising and lowering twice a day for the tides. In stormy weather, it is choppy whitecaps, but still no real waves.

Chapter 2

After picking through the can pile and only finding a couple of utensils, she decided she wanted to get as far from here as possible before dark. She wasn't sure what time of day it was, but dark would get here at some point. Since it is summer, there won't be extreme darkness and not last very long. But it is not like farther north where there is light 24/7 for a few months each summer.

As she walked, she straightened out the spoon she had found in the dump and it would do okay. The tines on the fork were not easily straightened and it looked like someone used it to pry something and then tossed when it bent. The small pieces of wire would come in handy to wire the fork to a longer branch to hold something over a fire to cook it. Everything would come in handy.

She tried to stay away from areas that would hold her footprints, not knowing if they would discover she was missing and come looking for her. The Devil's Club was always something to beware of and as she walked, she wondered how the old Shamans had made walking sticks from it. If that was one way to show how tough they were, it worked, and not just anyone would even try making anything useful from one.

After walking for quite a while, she figured she was far enough from the old camp that no one would smell fish cooking. She stopped and built a small fire from the dead twigs and duff she had been gathering as she walked.

She kept the fire small and under the overhanging boughs of a large evergreen to diffuse the smoke. While it burned, making a bed of coals, she cut the fish into fillets and then into strips.

Some willow branches would work as skewers and she threaded the strips on the branches, with each end stuck on a small limb to hold them in place. She figured the fish would keep better cooked or at least as dried as possible over the smoke than it would, fresh, in her pack.

The first ones were getting fairly well done as she finished skewering the last of the salmon strips so she ate several.

While she was eating, she noticed the sky was darkening and not only because she was under heavy timber and brush. The tree she was under would shed rain to a certain extend and she already had the fire heating some of the ground, so she unrolled George's coat and made herself a bed beside the fire so she could tend the fire and continue drying the fish strips overnight.

If it had been colder, she could have pulled the fire aside and snuggled into the warmed ground where the fire had been. She did pull some of the dirt back over the outside of the fire on the side away from her so it would hold some coals overnight and shield the glow from anyone at a distance.

Surprisingly, she fell asleep almost as soon as she relaxed. When she awoke some time later, she felt disoriented and couldn't figure out what had awakened her. As she listened, she felt almost as much as heard footsteps farther down the hill. The steps paused now and then, but did not alter course to come up the hill to her location.

After that, she held very still and tried to relax again, but didn't fall asleep again until just before daylight.

The sun in her eyes woke her up and she felt slightly sunburned. The bugs had made a feast on her face and she was swollen and itchy.

She stirred the coals a bit on her fire and it smoldered to life. Most of the fish strips were very dry, so she removed them from the sticks and stuffed them into a plastic bag in her pack. While she was sitting here, waiting for some water to heat in a can on the fire, she checked the broken strap and found it was not that difficult to repair. It only needed rethreaded through the buckles and rings.

By the time she had it repaired, she understood why it had been discarded. It was a royal pain to repair.

She added some of the berries she found near her sleeping area and steeped them in the hot water to have a morning drink. Then ate the berry remains when she finished the drink.

She made a handle for one of the stew cans from some of the short wire pieces and carried it while walking to pick more berries into.

When she came to a small creek, there were still some salmon moving up the creek with half of their backs out of the water. The fish would not be prime, but she was not in a position to be picky. Using the shovel, she scooped one out on the bank and grabbed onto it. It slipped right back into the creek.

She set her pack and other items aside farther and prepared to get serious about getting some fish.

Using the shovel, she scooped and threw the fish farther onto the bank and immediately grabbed the fish by the small area in front of the tail. She had a rock handy and smacked the fish on top the head to stun it, then cut the spine and tossed the fish farther up on the bank near her pack and went back for more.

Food might become a major problem later and she did not want to run out when it was so handy right now. When her arms got tired scooping fish, she started cleaning and filleting them, then cutting into strips and placing over brush and tree limbs. Then back to dipping. On one of her rest stops from dipping, she took her cans down to the beach and dipped some ocean water. It wasn't the best salt in the world, but dipping the strips in it before drying would add some saltiness to them.

If she could get these all dried, they would not take up as much room and the weight would be many times less. The second stew can she had packed some coals from her earlier fire in and damped down with some of the dirt, made it easy to start a fire to speed drying the catch. Having sunny days had to be taken advantage of, as it was very unusual in the Panhandle to have more than a couple of days in a row without rain showers, anyway.

One summer there was two full weeks with no rain and the town folks were worried they would have to start barging water over from the mainland.

A little ways back from the creek, she found a partial cave, where sometime in the past, high water had undercut a high bank. Trees grew over and around it and the water level had dropped or the creek had changed course to leave a fairly level floor in the cave.

It wasn't deep enough to worry about animals being denned up in it and this time of year, none denned anyway. She cut some poles with the knife and stuck some into the dirt partway up the walls and set the other end into the Y of another stick to build some drying racks.

Anya gathered as much firewood as she could find and stored it along the wall and in front of the open side of the cave. Then she started transferring the salmon strips to her new rack. The fire was easy to move on the shovel. When she went out front, she cut as many green boughs as she could carry and leaned them against the top of the cave opening to hold as much smoke inside the cave as possible for the fish. It also helped hide the cave entrance from casual viewers.

When she got back to the creek where she had caught the other fish, the run was down to just an occasional fish swimming by. She finally managed to flip one out to cook fresh for her evening meal. She was really going to hate fish after she got home. She didn't much like them at any time. At the moment, she was thankful for them.

Going back to the cave by a slightly different route, she found a nice patch of huckleberries, so came back with her cans and filled them full. She would try drying some of them, if she could figure out how without anything to spread them out on. When she got to the cave, she used her jacket and spread the berries in a thin layer on the jacket and hung it over the rack to dry a bit in the smoke. It was going to be well stained, but that was the least of her worries.

The night was uneventful and she awoke feeling quite rested. Having the fish and some berries drying made her feel more relaxed, also. She would rather proceed more slowly and eating well than to rush and starve.

Now that she was remembering the area she had walked, she didn't think it was the fish camp close to the end of the road on the island she lived on. She might be on another island or she might even be on the mainland. If she were on the mainland, she didn't have any idea how she would manage to get back home.

No matter what, the walking was not easy and she did not dare try walking along the beach out of the brush. She was lucky while walking, to be making more than 5 or 6 miles in an entire day.

So staying right here and preparing food for a possibly long trip yet ahead made sense. So she checked the creek yet again for fish and found a few more late ones making their way up the small stream. She managed to scoop out 4 more and cleaned them a bit farther away from the creek bank, then carried them up to her cave. She tried to not walk in the same areas more than once, but it was harder when she was staying right here for a few days.

Chapter 3

By the time the fish were dry enough to pack without spoiling, she was more than ready to leave the area. Yesterday, there was a lot of boat traffic near the beach and she thought maybe they were checking the burned shed. If only one body had been found in it, at least one person knew someone had got away and since George probably was already dead when he was left there, that left her.

Even though she was deep in the forest, she felt exposed and like there was a large target painted on her back.

While holed up in the cave, there had been a fairly good rain, but she thought she probably left enough tracks and trail through the brush that anyone could track her if they wanted to.

As she was leaving her cave, she spotted movement in the brush below and dropped to the ground. Slowly she peered through the leaves and saw a young black bear eating the fish remains where she had cleaned her fish. She hadn't even thought of the bears, and she had been sleeping right next to a good supply of fish. So far, she had been extremely lucky but that only goes so far and if she didn't start paying attention better, she could still end up dead.

As soon as she found a small dead spruce, she used her knife and whittled it down. Then she peeled off the rest of the bark and whittled the limbs all off. She sharpened both ends and tonight, when she had a fire, she would fire harden the points on the long stick. It was a primitive spear at best, but it might be just a bit better than none and gave her a feeling of confidence that she was planning ahead.

As she walked, she searched for food. Even though she had a fair supply of fish, she was not fond of fish and having to live on it was going to make her even less fond of fish. When she found the remains of a deer, she wanted to cut some meat from it, but the smell soon let her know it was beyond salvaging. As she skirted around it at a small distance, she saw that it had been partially buried so she walked a bit faster to get farther away as soon as possible without running.

That was probably a bear's cache and they do not enjoy sharing their food. She started watching even closer to make sure she didn't stumble into one by accident. Her spear and knives required close encounters and she really did not want that kind of closeness with anything right now. From reading, she knew how the Native people used to hunt bears with a spear. They would try to have a long spear and brace the butt end on the ground and hold it so the bear impaled itself on the spear. Somehow she could not see that working out very well for her. Only if it was a very small bear and then the mother would be somewhere right behind it.

As she considered all these possibilities, she was not aware of the sound of a motor chugging along somewhere just out of her sight near the beach.

When the sound did finally penetrate, she stopped and sat down. Not moving was her best disguise at present. She was still in the trees above the beach, but if anyone were looking at just the right moment, they might notice the movement of her clothing through the trees.

She could hear voices as the small boat moved along the shoreline. The words were indistinct, but the conversation sounded heated. Not again. One voice sounded familiar, but the other voice was different. Well, of course, since one of the others was probably dead or looked it when the boat pulled out with him draped over the edge a bit. This sounded like man #1 in another argument. He should pick his friends better or hang out in better company anyway.

The boat was still moving along, although slowly, so she stayed sitting on the hillside above them. The boat pulled up on the bank just a little farther down the beach from where she was sitting. They both got out of the boat and started carrying boxes from the boat up into the trees. She edged forward and was surprised to see a small cabin tucked back in the trees and not visible from just a few yards away, unless looked for and knowing it was there.

Somehow, she didn't think that cabin would show up on any property ownership papers or forest surveys.

Soon both men returned to the boat and left. She decided to do a little bit of snooping and found an outhouse deeper in the woods. Oh joy of joys, there was extra toilet tissue in a can, so she appropriated one roll. Leaves were better than nothing, but real TP was priceless.

Pushing her luck, she tried the back door and was surprised to find it unlocked. She quickly found the kitchen supplies and helped herself to a bag of salt and a couple of boxes of mac and cheese and some rice. She saw an open bag of new socks on a chair so helped herself to 2 pair. Several bottles of bug repellant caught her eye and she pocketed two of them. A lighter was on the floor and she picked it up also before going back outside.

A poncho was laying behind a bench by the back door, so she grabbed it too.

Her pack was going to be too heavy to carry if she kept adding to it, but she really missed having real food and anything but fish would be great.

If she could check some of the tidal pools at low tide, she might be able to find a crab or a few shrimp, but she was afraid to be out in the open that much. Even some of the seaweed would add a welcome change to her diet.

Anya knew goose grass and lambs quarters, also the wild chives. But she was not confident that she could tell the difference in the wild celery and water hemlock, so left anything resembling them alone. Surviving this much and then to poison herself was one of those little ironies she could do without.

She automatically picked anything that she knew as possible food as she walked. By the time she stopped each evening, she had enough to make an interesting sort of stew. Now she could add a little bit of rice to the pot each evening to give it more body and maybe make her feel like she actually had eaten.

While her dinner cooked, she soaked her feet in a small stream of water and indulged herself with a new pair of socks. They felt so good that she sat wriggling her toes in them, before finally putting her old boots on.

With the addition of the old poncho, she slept much warmer, wrapping it around her over George's coat and her jacket. Some moss mounded up over her and her pack made her difficult to see from any distance and also added warmth, so she slept very well that night.

Maybe too well. She awoke to the sound of voices. Not very close, but not all that far away, either. For being a huge unpopulated area of National forests, with very little private property available any where in or around it, there were sure a lot of people out and about.

She decided to just stay right where she was, everything was in under the moss with her, so no one should notice anything except maybe where she had pulled some of the moss loose. Usually that was done by a bear searching for grubs and roots to eat, if someone paid any attention to it. Except maybe to look around more in case the bear was still around.

She waited quite a while after the voices faded away before scooting out of her moss bed, rolling her gear, putting it into her pack and carefully leaving the area. She was trying very hard not to leave sign that a human had passed this way recently.

Her spear now had a fire hardened point on

each end. While her evening meal cooked, she heated the point and then rubbed it firmly against a rock, repeating until the tip looked like polished metal of some sort. It certainly wasn't as hard as metal, but it would still be enough to harvest a deer if she ever got close enough to one to try.

She cut other poles about the same size and practiced throwing them to try for some accuracy. She didn't want to throw her only fire hardened one and possibly either break or lose it. She was actually getting fairly good at throwing it and could hit a 5 inch circle quite regularly, if it wasn't too far away.

She walked for about an hour when she heard the rifle shot down below her. It is difficult to place a single shot, but no bullet thunked into the trees around her and she wasn't hit, so it wasn't intended for her. She realized she must be almost paralleling the people she heard earlier and was lucky she walked as quiet as possible through the woods and they had not heard her.

They must have been farther away than she thought, as she had not heard them either and now she wanted to see what they were shooting at.

Without another shot to place exact location, she proceeded with caution and it was well that she did. She heard the murmur of voices before she saw any sign of them.

The sound traveled uphill easily so she could make out a word once in a while.

It was definitely Man #1 again. She might not recognize his face if she saw him, but she would know his voice if she heard it. The other voice sounded familiar. Not of a friend, but someone she knew around town. They were complaining about some shipment and now without George, how were they supposed to manage?

George had been involved with these men? If they were making money, he sure never brought any of it home. He took odd jobs once in a while and worked for anyone needing an extra hand on their fishing boat, but he really didn't like having a steady daily job. If she wasn't so good at scrounging wild food and growing a good garden, they would have starved long ago depending on his work ethic.

If he was working with these men, he must have been either spending what he earned on his girlfriend she wasn't supposed to know about, or he was using drugs again. He drank, but usually not very often. She wished she could just ask them.

As she listened to them talk, she was horrified to learn they were setting up meth labs all through the woods on the islands. She knew many people grew a bit of weed for their own use, but these fellows planned on planting on a very large scale through the woods. They were bringing in illegal helpers and planning on setting up migrant camps in under the canopy of trees covering most of the islands.

They were using some of the fishing boats to haul groceries up from the Seattle area so no one was buying a large quantity of food locally. Everyone was dressing in camo clothing and the tent housing was also military surplus, so blended right into the trees.

She was not that surprised to hear the drug people were targeting the wilderness in Alaska. With no road system to speak of and a very low population, it was the perfect area for lowlife scum suckers to congregate.

It's pluses were also minuses in some ways. New people would stand out and everyone would notice them so it made sense to hide them out in the woods with the set-up they were going to be building. Anyone buying extra food in the amounts these people would be needing, would be the subject of conjecture and conversations all over the islands in a short time. The population may be small but they are snoopy. Farther North, they call it the mukluk telegraph.

Everyone leaves you alone if that is what you want, but they seem to always know everything that is going on. It's a great place to live.

As she listened, Man #1 was still upset over her being killed as she was an innocent bystander, not even involved. Things like that would draw attention to the area and lack of attention was what they were counting on to make this work out.

Chapter 4

The men were dressing out a deer they had shot. When she got to a point where she could see and hear them, she sat down again.

They soon had the meat ready to load on their backpacks and set off back the direction they came from.

After they had been gone for quite a while, she went down to the butchering site and salvaged the hide and some of the organ meats they left behind. She could not be choosy now and heart and liver were both edible meats. The lower legs were still attached to the hide, so she would skin them out later. She just wanted to get away from this area.

The hike back up the hill took a lot longer than coming down did and she was feeling the affects of adrenalin leaving her. Once she got high enough on the hill and made it over a small stream where she refilled all her bottles, she stopped and started a small fire.

The smell of cooking meat would drift a long ways on air currents, so she wanted to make sure she had at least part of a hill between her and the men before she started cooking. Thin slivers of meat roasted over a small fire on a stick should cook very fast and she would eat them as fast as they cooled enough to eat. So she hoped no one would wonder where the scent originated. She didn't want it to last on the air any longer than necessary.

The red meat was so satisfying, she cooked and ate more than she should after not having any for so long. It was so fresh, she figured she would have some stomach upset later.

She cleaned up her little area, trying to make it not show someone had a fire there recently. The burned stones were turned over so the fresh char wouldn't show. Dirt sprinkled over the ashes and moss dribbled over that, to blend it in. A casual glance would not notice it at all.

Her next stop was just before dark and rain was threatening. She found some large old evergreen trees growing very close together and made herself a small shelter in under the overhanging branches. It should shed most rain and would make her night much more comfortable.

She built another small fire carefully so she didn't set her shelter on fire and cooked more of the fresh meat. It would not keep very well so she sliced it all very thin and started drying the heart slices on sticks set a little ways from the fire but close enough to help speed the drying.

She cooked the rest of the slivers of liver and then started drying them, also. She might be able to tell herself the heart was just jerky, but raw liver was just something she didn't want to try eating yet.

By morning, the rain was settled in and doing very well. She decided to stay in her snug camp and continue drying the meat slices. She worked on the deer hide all day while feeding the fire small bits of wood. She soon had the hide well fleshed and was stretching and working it as it dried. It wouldn't be tanned, but it would be one more layer to use as a sleep mat and help her keep from losing body heat to the ground.

The deer in Southeast Alaska are very small, but it would still be better than no mat under her at all. The lower leg pieces she would try to make some moccasins or mittens. They were small enough she would be lucky to make much except rawhide laces out of them.

The fillet knife was very sharp, so she wedged it into part of a dead tree and started cutting a long strip from one of the front leg pieces. By turning the piece of hide, she was able to make one very long thin strip out of the small leg. It was working so well, she did the other front leg piece that way, also. There were always uses for strong ties. She trimmed another long strip from around the edges of the main hide so she could braid the little strips and have a piece of rawhide rope. That would make it much stronger if she needed it. She rubbed most of the hair off the strips by rubbing them back and forth on the fillet blade back while it was still stuck in the tree.

The rope wasn't very long, but it was more than she had before, so she was happy with it. She coiled it and tied it on her pack. She would work it every evening to soften it and make it more pliable.

By the third morning, the rain had stopped and the sun was shining. Everything was still dripping and she would be soaked as soon as she started walking. It looked like it would be a fairly warm day, so she set out anyway. She would soon be steaming as she dried while walking. Cleaning up camp took a little more time than usual since she had been there longer than most of her camps.

When she stopped for a break and to eat a salmon strip, a raven perched on a branch nearby and kept making small chortling noises as though he were communicating with her. It looked quite young. She talked a bit to him and he seemed very interested. She tossed a small piece of her salmon to him and he gulped it down after another brief dialogue. He had better manners than some of the guys she knew.

As she walked the rest of the day, he would show up and land up ahead of her and seemed to be pointing out which way she should go if she was in doubt. She figured he had just as much idea where she was going as she did, so allowed him to lead.

When she stopped for the night, he landed nearby and waddled over to inspect her campsite. As she ate some of the liver slices, she tossed him a small piece of the liver, also. She cooked some rice and crumbled up more liver into the rice for her own version of dirty rice. A few wild chives added more flavor and the bit of salt made it a very good meal. She made some rice balls to save for breakfast and tossed one to the raven. He picked at it then gulped it down, made a sound she interpreted as thanks and left. Yeah, eat and run.

The raven woke her with agitated squawks fairly early and she packed her gear, then moved deeper into the trees. She soon heard the sound of a helicopter coming in at a very low elevation. Through the limbs, she could see that it was not a police chopper and she did not recognize the symbol on the sides. It flew just above the tree tops and followed the lower valleys so no one could really see it from very far away even if they were looking for it.

She figured it was with the men planning

the drug kingdom. It would give them a way
to transport their product. Maybe they
planned on taking it into Canada from here,
since that was closer and maybe smuggling it
into the States from there. Either way, if they
saw her, she probably would have a very short
life expectancy.

While she crouched in the trees, she saw that
they were looking for something below, using
binoculars. They would sweep back and forth
in a grid pattern and suddenly they turned
and went down toward the beach. She heard
several shots then silence.

She and the raven shared her rice balls and
sat under the trees for a while. The sound of
the motor slowly died out as it moved farther
off and now she would try to be listening for
it.

Curiosity got the best of her and she slowly
made her way down to the beach. She knew
the general area the shots had been fired near,
so she came to the edge of the trees only a
small ways from a still form laying in the edge
of a small stream running into the ocean.

She edged over near it and watched for a
while but did not see any sign of movement
from it or around in the area. It was only a
few feet from the trees, so she stayed in the
trees until she could practically reach out and
touch the man sprawled out on the gravel.

She carefully reached out and touched his

hand. It was still warm, so she grasped his wrist and pulled as hard as she could, to move him on into the trees a bit.

He groaned as she moved him and she almost lost her grip on his wrist. Moving him without checking him over first was probably not the best thing to do, but she did not want to move out into the sight of anyone near the beach.

Once she had him entirely into the trees, she reached out with a tree branch and wiped gravel over the dark smear of blood left on the place he had been laying. A fine drizzle was falling now and soon would wash away the blood smear from her moving him.

Once they were farther back in the trees, she turned him over and saw that it was Man #1 from the boat. Now why would they be shooting at him?

She pulled his shirt aside and it looked like one bullet had grazed along his ribs and another had just creased his head. He should survive the gunshots if she could help him stay hidden from his shooters.

That was the trouble with people using the semiautomatic weapons. They never learned to actually aim and shoot, they sprayed and prayed they would hit something and wasted a lot of bullets doing it. In his case, it saved his life for the moment. She had no idea whether they would come check to make sure he was dead or just leave him lay and hope the wilderness got him.

She used a piece of her precious TP to cover his wounds as it would help keep them from bleeding more. Then she covered the one on his side with his handkerchief from his pocket and tied it in place with some of her rawhide strips. The one on his head would just have to make do with the TP over it and his hat which she retrieved with a stick.

She checked him over for weapons of any sort, retrieving a handgun from his belt and a knife from a neck holster, besides the pocket knife . She removed his wallet and set it aside.

She used the small stream to wash his face off and he started coming around. She wasn't sure of his intentions toward her and was hesitant to stay and let him see her, but figured she could outrun him at the moment, anyway.

She sat back away from him as he came around, just out of his reach.. She held his own gun on him as he tried to sit up. He slowly eased into a sitting position, holding his head with both hands as though he were afraid it might fall off. She imagined his headache probably made it feel like it would.

He mumbled something, but she couldn't understand what he was trying to say. Then she heard him say something about his boat.

She wasn't sure if he meant he had one stashed somewhere along this section of beach or what, so she asked him, "What boat?"

He jerked at the sound of another voice, and turned toward her. He squinted through the pain, trying to make her out in the dim shadows under the brush she was sitting in.

"My boat should be in the mouth of the creek, with some brush pulled over it."

"Why were those people shooting at you?" she asked.

He hesitated and she thought, he is trying for a reasonable lie.

"They mistook me for a deer?"

"You might want to work on your story a little bit, if that is all you can come up with."

He turned more toward her and the pulling at the bullet crease along his ribs startled a gasp out of him. His hand went to his side and he could feel her makeshift dressing of his wound. He gingerly touched his head and she told him he should be careful and not start it bleeding again.

The raven shifted on his perch near her head and she spoke low soothing words to the bird. The man was starting to think she and the bird were both figments of his imagination, but his own gun still pointed in his general direction put the note of reality in the situation. He didn't know how long it had been since the shots were fired, but he felt an urgency about leaving this area as soon as possible.

"You do know those people will be coming back to check on me, don't you? We should all be gone before they get here."

"You never answered my question, why were they shooting at you in the first place?"

"I'm guessing there has been a turnover in management of the firm working here. I worked with the old management, new management doesn't trust me."

Okay, that made sense in an odd way. She stood up to go see if she could find his boat. He tried to stand and she told him to rest until she found it, then he could knock himself out trying to get around if he wanted to.

The small creek they were beside widened out and made a very small bay at it's mouth. His boat was pulled up as close to the trees as possible and tied off to a stump. It had a small cabin in the middle but was a very small boat for an ocean craft. She untied the line and walked it into the trees, scraping the bottom as she proceeded. She worked it around until it was pointing back out toward the ocean, then tied it off again to go get the man.

She squeaked as he staggered out onto the bank beside her. She was still carrying her pack and had his wallet and gun in her pockets.

She helped him into the boat and it now rested firmly on the bottom. She yanked and pulled until she got him ungrounded, then a bit farther, before joining him on the boat.

He started the motor and she recognized that it was very deceiving in appearances. That was the sound of a high performance engine.

Chapter 5

Once they were out on the open water, he opened it up and they were fairly flying over the small whitecaps the wind had blown up. It looked like a storm was moving in and she dreaded having to find shelter from it. Good or bad, she had thrown in her lot with this stranger that was upset when he thought she had been killed although he evidently worked in the drug trade.

Great, George had a lot of faults, but until recently, they were faults she could deal with and live with. She didn't have a clue what this man had in mind and she didn't want to try a swim to any bank from here.

The fine spray felt like ice needles against her face as they sped along and she soon realized she had not been on the island she thought she was.

She would never have reached a town or community. The old abandoned fish camps and once in a while sign of an abandoned logging area was all she saw as they proceeded.

About the time she was feeling sorry that she had not even got to say goodbye to her friendly raven, the boat started slowing down.

They were easing in to another small stream on another island. He placed his fingers to his lips to signal quiet and she was happy to comply.

As they came around another corner in the stream, it widened out a little bit and he eased over to the bank. She was up and out of the boat before he even shut down the motor. He tossed her the line and she tied it off to a handy stump.

After he got out, he pulled the back end of the boat toward the bank after turning it around, and tied it snuggly also, then started pilling brush and sticks around it to hide it's outline from casual observation.

As they were covering the boat, he whispered, "By the way, my name is Philip Buldock. What's yours?"

"Anya Carpenter."

"YOU are George's wife, er, widow?"

"Yes."

He remained silent for quite a while, sorting through just what he could say. "I'm sorry."

"What? Sorry I am his widow or sorry he is dead and I am a widow now?"

He was at a loss for words and anything he might say now would be easily taken the wrong way, so he remained quiet.

In a few minutes, she finally said she was sorry for saying that, she just isn't used to being a widow yet and still trying to make sense of the last few weeks. This is the first time she actually realized she is now a widow,.

She heard a familiar chortling sound and looking into the trees above them, spotted a raven. It surely couldn't be her raven friend, but it certainly acted like it. It hopped down to the ground and waddled over to her. Peering up and trilling little inquiries. She reached in her pack and pulled out her leftover rice balls from last night's dinner and tossed the raven one.

Phillip held out his hand and she tossed one to him also while munching on the last one herself.

"Say, these are really good. What all is in them?"

"Rice, slivers of dried cooked liver, wild chives and a bit of seaweed."

"No wonder he followed along if you have been feeding him this stuff, it is good."

Okay, he got points for saying that. She checked his ID in his wallet before finally giving it back to him. It even matched the name he had given her. She still had his gun and knives in her pockets.

He put his wallet in his pocket and didn't say anything about the rest. She felt slightly guilty, but not enough to trust him with them, just yet.

They climbed up a steep hill until they

reached an open area closer to the top. Then he pointed out the direction of town and some of the landmarks she should look for. He told her it would be far better if she were not seen with him.

She figured maybe he didn't want his employers or whoever they were, to see him with George's widow that was supposed to be dead, too.

He said No, she would be an immediate target, if she came in with him. Since the shooting on the beach, he figured he had a target on his back for someone. It would probably go for anyone with him, also. He handed her a small canister and asked if she got to town and he wasn't anywhere around, to please give that to someone that would come and ask for it.

She handed it back and said she would not be part of anything to do with drugs or illegal activity. He looked at her strangely, then handed it back and said it was to go to his mother and he didn't send drugs to his Mom.

She slid the little canister into her pocket with his gun. She was still undecided about the gun and he told her to keep it, she was going to have to still do a lot of walking and he had the boat. She gave him back his knives since she did have knives.

He faded back into the brush as she started hiking down the other side of the hill. She did not see him or even any movement from him as she walked on down into the tree line.

She found a overhanging rock outcropping and set up her camp for the evening under it. She would have a good view around her area and she could screen her fire from anyone seeing it from a distance.

For the first time on this whole trek, she felt alone, this evening. Somehow in the short time she traveled with Philip, she got used to having him around. She prepared her dinner and shared some with the raven that was perched on a rock near her.

He patiently waited while the rice cooked, but got impatient for it to cool enough for him to eat. He would hop back and forth from one foot to another, chirruping with increasing agitation until she decided it was cool enough not to hurt him.

His eating habits were not dainty, but then, George's hadn't been either. So it felt normal to be feeding a messy bird. However, the raven did clean up after himself, then sat and preened his feathers to make sure he was clean and hadn't missed any of his dinner.

She banked the fire and prepared her sleeping area. The raven watched a bit then flew off to find his own perch for the night. There were noises during the night that she could not recognize and she wondered if she were far enough from any well used trails not to be found by the smell of her smoke.

When she awoke, she used water from one of her bottles to heat for a morning tea to start the day. She had some dried huckleberries yet and they were tasty as tea. She scattered her small fire and broke up the coals to make sure they were really out. Not knowing where her next water was going to be found made her hesitant about using her drinking water for the fire.

Anya already had her pack on and was starting into the trees when she heard voices. She immediately turned away from the sound and started hiking faster than she planned. Her foot slipped on a loose rock under the moss and she went tumbling down into a small ravine.

After she stopped rolling, she was totally disoriented and seeing stars a bit, so held very still. Luckily, her pack was still with her and nothing seemed to be broken that she could tell when she tried moving toes and fingers. She heard someone laugh and say they must have scared a bear, as much noise as it made getting out of the area. Then the voices faded into the distance.

Once she was sure they were gone, she tried sitting up. She felt a bit dizzy and when she touched her head, she found a painful area that felt sticky. There was some blood on her hand when she looked at it. Her cheekbone was sore, also, so must have found some rocks on her way down. She remained seated for quite a while before her stomach settled and her head felt like it would probably stay on her shoulders if she tried standing.

About halfway to her feet, she wasn't so sure. Then she put all her weight on her right foot and her ankle rebelled. She lowered herself back to the ground and looked over her surroundings.

She was in a fairly narrow ravine that showed evidence of runoff water washing through if there were heavy rains. On the other side, there was a mossy overhang with a tree on it that made it look like it might collapse any minute or shelter assorted wild animals.

She hobbled over to it, using her spear to hold most of her weight from her right foot. It was a few feet higher than the floor of the ravine, so even if water did rush down through it, maybe it wouldn't reach this high.

When she stooped to go under the moss, there was a fairly large area underneath that looked almost dry. She couldn't stand upright in it, but there was plenty of room to spread out her belongings and have a small fire.

Someone in the past must have used it also as there was a pile of dry firewood against the back wall. The walls appeared to be mostly rock with a slab over the ceiling holding it all up. A person could be quite cozy if they enclosed the front opening a bit with something.

She sat near the opening and looked the area over. There were some rocks scattered around, so she started moving the ones she could reach without standing and placing them under the overhang to shield a fire when she wanted to cook, inside. She pushed a bit of the dirt up against the rocks on the inside so no light would show through. She did leave a peep hole near the top that she could see out if she heard anything or before stepping outside.

That worked so well for one side, she decided to do the other side the same and leave the middle for her entrance.

It helped pass the day and she didn't feel like she was wasting time just sitting around, waiting to heal up enough to walk on out. Then she spotted a patch of sour grass and scooted on down to pick enough for dinner.

There were some ferns in the bottom of the ravine, so she gathered some and crushed them to wrap around her ankle to sooth it a bit.

There were berries on the bank above her, but she figured it would not help her ankle heal if she kept getting on it all the time. They would still be okay, she hoped, when she could stand. Then as she needed to relieve herself and had to maneuver around for that, she used that as an excuse to pick all the berries she could reach while leaning against the bank of moss. There were more than she could eat with her dinner, so she started some drying to carry with her.

Chapter 6

When Anya woke up the next morning, she still felt a bit of a headache and her ankle was still sore and stiff, but not as bad as yesterday. She did some stretches while still laying down to keep her ankle from tightening up. Then she turned her head a few times, trying to find some position that didn't ache as bad. She finally gave up on that and got up.

She rolled her bedding and repacked it. She tried to always have her pack ready to go at a moments notice just in case she had to leave and didn't want to lose her small amount of possessions. So far, she had enough to survive with and didn't want to try surviving on less.

The pack was kept just inside the "doorway" of her shelter, so it was easy to grab the straps if she had to try getting away. She really didn't think her ankle would be much good in an escape, but she would try anyway, if she had to. The crushed ferns felt so good on her ankle, she kept some handy to add as the old ones dried out and lost their coolness.

Her water supply was running low, so she hoped she could leave here by tomorrow. It was a nice shelter, but the lack of available water was a drawback. When she went for a few more ferns, she was stabbing the ground with her spear and found a damp spot so dug it out a bit with her piece of shovel. Water seeped in, but was very muddy. If she had to stay longer, she could use it.

The next morning, her ankle still was not up to an all day hike, so she decided to spend at least one more day here. The water seep would keep her in water and she was pleasantly surprised to find it was clear and not bad tasting. She refilled all her bottles and dragged her pack back to the shelter.

The raven showed up that evening and she again shared her dinner with him. Now they were almost out of the liver pieces, so were back to using mostly dried salmon with their rice. The raven didn't mind at all. He was good to cook for, never complained about the menu.

Raven was waiting for her when she came out of the shelter in the morning. Her ankle was felling pretty good and she thought maybe one more day would see it back to good as new.

She shared breakfast with the raven and they discussed that days jobs to be done. Well, she murmured to him and he chortled to her. She didn't want her voice to carry for anyone else to hear, so seldom spoke above a low murmur to the raven. Whispers carry better over a distance than most people realize.

She walked up the ravine a little ways and found a lot more berries, so picked as many as she had room for to carry and as many as she could eat as she picked. The pack was unwieldy for berry picking, but she was not going to leave it behind.

Since she tucked any used paper under moss as she used it, it would just look like scat from a bear as the diets were about the same. The berries would add realism.

She and the raven started back to the shelter when the raven suddenly spooked and took off flying. She did not wait to see why, she dove in behind some brush and sat very still with Philip's gun in her hand. Soon she heard steps coming up the ravine.

She was surprised to see Philip step into view. When he was even with her position in the brush, she softly called, "Philip."

He tensed, then slowly looked around. He did not spot her until she moved. Then he came over and sat down next to her. She had stuck his handgun down at her side when she realized who it was.

"I was getting worried when you had not made it back to town. Are you okay?"

"Yes, just slipped and hurt my ankle and was giving it time to heal up before heading back out"

"I brought you some more rice. You would probably rather have something else, but it is the easiest to carry and fills a person up. With other stuff added, it makes a pretty good meal. I included a bag of jerky and some pepperoni sticks, too. I still think it is risky to show up with me, so I will head back. Where are you staying?"

"You came right by my shelter, so I must have done it right."

He wanted to see how she was managing and was surprised when she showed him her shelter. She had been picking up sticks to add to the firewood pile as she walked, so he was, also. She wanted to leave it stocked as it had been when she found it, but in better shape for staying in.

He unpacked supplies from his bag and several bottles of water for her. She could stay here several more days now and let her ankle heal up completely. That would give her berries time to dry, also. She was starting to like having the berry tea for breakfast. She was drying some of the leaves to use as tea with the fruit.

She asked Philip if he would go by her place and see if it was still okay and her rent was paid up until the end of next month, so it should still be hers. He wasn't sure whether everyone thought she was dead or not, so said he would look into it for her.

He told her when he was on his way into the boat harbor the other day from dropping her off, someone tried to ram his boat. He didn't get the numbers off the boat as they had something over them. If his boat wasn't so souped up, they would have succeeded in sinking his boat and probably him with it.

It would be easy to say they were trying to fish him out of the water while actually holding him under with poles. They could do it in front of witnesses on the banks and no one could tell from a distance.

He was glad she was okay, and he would start back now and camp overnight along the way. His boat was stashed at the mouth of the little stream that begins just down the hill from this ravine.

Anya decided she would just stay put a few more days. Now she had some food and a bit of variety, not a lot, but it was welcome. She started out by eating a pepperoni stick. The flavor was delicious and she savored every bite until the raven showed up and then she shared it with him. He wasn't savoring, he was gulping, so only got a few bites.

She shredded a piece of jerky to add to their rice and some of the wild greens she found on her berry picking trip. It would add different flavor than the salmon, anyway.

Once she got home, she was going to bake

some potatoes and indulge, big time. Rice is good, but every meal is just a bit too much. If she started thinking of what she wanted to eat, then she would only get depressed, so she stopped that and got on with surviving out here and enjoying what she did have. She was totally surprised to find several dark chocolate candy bars stuck in the bottom of the bag with the rice and jerky. That was not going to be shared with the raven and probably was not good for him, anyway. She would keep telling herself that, anyway.

Anya gave herself 3 more days to recover fully and she felt that she was, when she packed up to leave on the fourth morning. She had the wood pile nicely stacked against the back wall, the shelter walls nicely built up with stones on both sides of the entrance in front and everything brushed out from the inside to leave it nice for the next person needing or wanting to use it. She left a couple of bottles of water and one of her washed out peanut butter jars full of rice, set in one of her cooking cans, on a niche up in the wall, also.

Chapter 7

As Anya walked, she noticed more ripe berries and some already over ripe showing that summer was nearing an end. She was glad she had not needed to make this trip in winter. Her diet would have been starvation rations, since she was afraid to go along the beaches.

Anya knew there were more wild foods available, but not being sure just what was safe to eat and what wasn't, she hesitated to try any of the unknown plants, no matter how good they looked. That would be a priority after she got home.

When she got down the hill closer to the ocean, she started paying closer attention to boat traffic. There seemed to be a lot of small fishing boats meandering around but not in the usual way fishing boats operated.

It was more as though they were searching for something. She found an area she could see the ocean without being seen easily herself and watched them for a while. It appeared they were searching a grid and she wondered if someone had gone missing or a boat had sunk.

After her brief stop, she continued on toward her house. She would probably have to camp tonight, but should make it home tomorrow. She did not want to think about the possibility that she would still be in danger after she got home. She didn't know anything and couldn't recognize anyone from her kidnapping.

She would play as dumb as a box of rocks and hope everyone left her alone. She didn't have any strategy beyond that.

The raven continued to accompany her and stayed near as she camped that evening. She splurged on the amount of rice she cooked and added enough dried fish to make it actually have some flavor, then threw in some pieces of the pepperoni to spice it up a little bit. It wouldn't win any taste tests, but by now, it was very satisfying and filling. She spread out enough to cool for the raven and let hers cool some in the can, rolled his into small balls and shared her dinner with him.

She spread out the fire and let it warm the ground a bit, then let it die out, spread her bedding over the warmed ground and went to sleep.

Anya procrastinated a bit about getting started the next morning. Now that she was so close to home, she was apprehensive about what she would find waiting for her once she arrived.

George was dead, and through no fault of her own, she had missed work with no notice, so she doubted if she still had a job. Work was hard to find on an island.

Some of her artwork sold at the local gift shop to the summer tourists, but she doubted if she had much coming in from that and summer tourist season was almost over. No more cruise ships would be putting in to port after September. She wasn't sure, but thought it must be close to September now. She lost track of days and didn't know how long she had been unconscious to start with.

She did know she had paid 2 months ahead on their rent all the time without telling George. He tended to neglect to share his checks and she didn't want to be evicted. She would let her landlord know as soon as she got home.

She still stayed above the beach and soon was above the end of the road from town. There were some vehicles parked there, but she didn't recognize any, so continued on as she was going.

It still took her several hours to reach her house, on the outskirts of town. The brush is so dense in some areas, it is almost impossible to go through so going around is usually easier. Then she wasn't paying close enough attention and got into some Devil's Club and would be picking stickers out for a long time.

Anya came down to her house from the back and found the key she kept hidden near the back door. She let herself into the house and was dismayed to see that it had been trashed in her absence. The phone was torn off the wall and it took her a while to rewire it enough to try using it.

She immediately called her landlord to tell him someone had trashed the house. He said he would be right over.

She found her small digital camera in the bedroom under her clothes that had been dumped out of the drawers. She took pictures of each room and tried not to disturb anything before someone else saw what it looked like.

A knock at the door startled her, but she checked, saw her landlord and let him in. He looked at her like she was a ghost. She knew she didn't look her best, but she didn't think she was that bad.

"Dang, girl, you have lost a lot of weight and where the heck have you been?"

Another knock at the door proved to be the town police officer. She let him in and then sat them down after they righted the chairs and told them what had happened since she last saw them. The officer was recording it and asked her a few questions now and then. She did not mention Philip's name. Nor did she mention that she now had a gun. It didn't seem like a need to know requirement.

Her landlord, Red Dutcher, said George's remains had been located, but they were not sure of his identity until now. Everyone thought she and he had just taken off, but since their stuff was still here and no plane tickets purchased, he kept the house ready if they came back. She still had 2 weeks paid up on her rent.

As far as he knew, no one had been hired in her place at the store, so maybe if she told them what happened, she would still have her job. The officer, Joel Jamieson, said he would verify it with them for her.

Anya asked if she could start cleaning up her house and see if anything was missing. Joel thought it was probably kids that heard no one was home. She didn't think so, since she had been removed from this house when she was kidnapped. He agreed, there was that.

They helped her right the furniture in each of the rooms and she said it didn't look like anything was missing. They never had anything worth stealing anyway and most thieves would take pity and bring them something better.

Even the keys were found to their old pickup that was still sitting out front. The TV and player were broken, but hadn't worked very well anyway, so was not a great loss. Her art supplies were still on the shelves, but they were easy to see that nothing else was in or around them.

There were no fresh groceries and stuff was growing in the fridge, so she didn't even want to think what it was going to take to clean it.

Red offered to come back in an hour and take her in to buy groceries and see if she still had a job or not. She realized she probably smelled pretty bad and looked even worse, so after the men left and she locked both doors and checked the windows, she found enough clean clothes on the floor and took a long hot shower.

When she stepped outside, the raven landed on the porch railing and she went in and got him a couple of the salmon strips. He looked her over closely, then accepted the salmon.

Her elderly neighbor was watching and came over. He said he was glad to see her and that she was okay. It was a good thing to feed the raven. Ravens were important to the Native peoples in Alaska and it showed she had a good heart. The raven hopped down onto the porch and waddled over to sit near her as the old man talked and he said that she must belong to the Raven Clan.

She told the man that the raven had accompanied her for most of her trip. The old man patted her hand and said she should be careful, the people that trashed her house might come back. She put Philips gun in her pocket when Red came to give her a ride to the store.

She understood by Red and the old man showing support for her, that they believed her and would be a help in the days to come.

Her boss at the store was not too friendly at first, then changed to incredulous and then accepted her back and her shift would start tomorrow. He had been trying to find someone he could rely on to fill the job, but no one applied that he would trust in his store handling money. He handed her the pay she had coming from the few days before she was kidnapped and told her welcome back.

The manager at the gift shop was happy to see her and had a fairly large check for her from the end of tourist season. Her paintings and other items she made sold well this year. She immediately paid Red 2 months rent just to see her through in case she didn't make enough on her part time job.

When she got home, the raven was still on her porch. She tugged and pulled until she got George's old broken down armchair out onto the porch and put some salmon pieces on it. The raven hopped right up into it and settled in to eat. She went inside to heat up something for her own dinner.

Later, she heard the neighbor's dog barking and when she checked outside, a car had pulled up near the old man's house. Philip was one of the men that got out of the car and the old man welcomed them inside. Then she heard an odd bark outside and discovered the raven imitating the dog. She laughed and tossed him another treat. She had a flying watch dog.

Soon, there was a tapping at her back door. She went to the door and asked who it was.

"It's Philip, may I come in?"

She opened the door and he slipped in. Her shades were drawn, so no one outside could see in. She turned out the kitchen light anyway. He stayed just inside the back door and told her he had to hurry, he was only supposed to be using the outhouse at the old man's. He told her to trust no one and be very careful. Then he kissed her forehead and left.

When she got up the next morning, she showered and rushed getting ready for work. She wasn't even sure her old pickup would start, after sitting so long. It was always tempermental anyway and it might just decide it liked retirement.

She was pleasantly surprised when it actually started on the third try. Then she heard a faint ticking sound and after the last few weeks, she was paranoid enough to bail out and hit the ground running. She almost made it to the house when the old truck blew.

The force of the blast knocked her down and she was dazed for a bit, not sure whether she should try to get up or stay put.

Soon she heard a siren and decided to stay put for the moment. Great, just freaking great. Now how was she supposed to get to work?

The town firetruck pulled in and the police car right behind it. Joel came over where she was sitting on the ground and asked if she needed a ride to be checked over at the hospital. She told him, No, she needed a ride in to work.

"That can be arranged. Looks like not everyone is happy to see you made it home."

"I really don't know what to do. That pickup was the only thing of any value that I own and I have no way of buying another. It was insured, but is so old, it only had liability on it."

Joel told her he would ask around and see if anyone had another older vehicle at a very reasonable price and let her know. Then he gave her a ride to work.

Anya figured she could walk to and from work if she knew she needed to. Nothing in town was all that far away and after all the walking she had been doing the last few weeks, it should be easy.

Chapter 8

On her lunch break, Sandy, from the gift shop she sold her artwork through, came over to see her.

"I was wondering if you could do some extra pieces for me to add to my show I am putting on in Juneau next month."

"Did you have anything in mind?"

"No, maybe just something Alaskan themed. The show is going to be televised and some will be sold on-line as it is being shown."

"Oh wow, that would be too perfect. After the morning I have had, I needed something positive."

"You had a bad morning?"

"Yes, my pickup blew up as I was getting ready to come to work."

"As in blew the motor or really blew up?"

"Really blew up, I heard some ticking and jumped out and then it blew all over the place."

"Girl, you should move into town, maybe just rent the little apartment over my garage if you want, for a while. It would be easier to get to work without a vehicle and you could just help out in my shop for the rent and I would pay you to handle the shop while I am at the show In Juneau."

That sounded too good to be true, but she could not see a downside in it, except the pesky one of having already paid 2 more months in advance on her rent out where she was living now. She wasn't too sure how she would like living in the middle of town. It isn't a large town, but it is still a town.

The sign in the middle of the boat harbor said it all, "Welcome, Home to 2000 Happy Souls and 500 Sore Heads." She wasn't sure which category she would fall into.

Sandy asked her to think it over and see what she could do for some art pieces to show in the Juneau show. It would get her more name recognition for her work.

While she worked at the store that afternoon, she was thinking of what to make for the show. The raven kept flitting across everything she thought of until she gave in and concentrated on how to use the raven as her main theme and do a series around him. On her break, she sketched several quick small thumbnail sketches to get her ideas on paper before she forgot some of them.

One of the other employees lived past her house, so she caught a ride home with her after work. She even brought home a small bag of dog food to give the raven every day, if he stuck around.

He waddled out to meet her as she walked up the driveway, both giving the demolished pickup a wide berth. Then he ambled alongside her to the house, mumbling and occasionally barking. He really enjoyed imitating the yappy dog and she wasn't sure how any neighbors would react to her barking companion.

She snapped several pictures of him from various sides and poses so she could use them as reference for accuracy in her work. She didn't have internet, but she did have an old laptop and a printer so she could work on the pictures for various effects, also.

After an evening meal eaten on the porch and some of hers poured over some of the dog food for the raven, She set up her easel and started sketching out a large canvas to paint. Then she quickly painted in the deep shadows in Gesso to start the depth she wanted to portray in the finished picture. As soon as she had one ready to dry, she started another and soon had several lined up around the walls in the house.

She painted the entire under painting in black or white gesso and then would layer thin layers of oils over to build up a painting that on the surface looked very realistic, but as you looked, it gained depth and nuances that usually are not noticed in nature.

By the time she was satisfied with the beginnings of the pictures, it was well after midnight and she was glad she didn't have to work this morning.

She started in again, as soon as she finished breakfast. The backgrounds were painted in and the ravens were shown in all their playful or serious moods. Their deep black feathers were painted, then overlaid with sheer coats of lavenders and teal to shimmer with their iridescence, subtle yet intriguing.

Late that afternoon, she and the raven went for a walk along the beach. She needed a break and he needed to be a raven. He flew in circles and played in the edge of the water, picking up shiny pieces of rock and carrying it until he found one he liked better. Anya enjoyed her walk and the raven seemed to be having fun also.

When she returned to the house, there was red paint smeared all across her door and front window. She went around to the back and unlocked the back door to go in. She called the landlord and the police and waited for them to arrive. She also called Sandy and asked if the apartment over the garage was still available and was it the one with the deck over part of the garage? Sandy said yes on all counts. She asked if she could bring a dumpy old armchair to put on the deck in case her friend the raven decided to join her, living in town.

Sandy laughed and said she didn't mind at all. Red was upset that she was having so many problems and offered her rent back, since it looked like it was going to be dangerous to her and not so great on his property either, for her to continue living there.

Joel was driving his own pickup when he answered the call, and then offered to load some of her stuff and deliver it to Sandy's if she wanted it moved right now.

She did. They loaded the old chair much to the raven's displeasure. Then she loaded all her artwork and supplies in the back with the chair, happy that it was a lull in the daily showers common this time of year.

Her duffle bag was still packed and it didn't take long to pack the rest of her belongings that were salvaged from the last time her house was vandalized. She thought it looked pretty pitiful, that the raven and her art supplies took up more room in the truck than her other personal belongings.

Sandy's deck on the garage roof was partly roofed over, so the raven's chair was placed just under the roof so the raven would have free access if he felt like joining her. Part of the deck was glassed in, so she set up her artwork out in that area. The light was good and there were plenty of electric lights to use if natural light wasn't enough. It would make an ideal studio. As Sandy helped her set her paintings around the area, she said the raven paintings would steal the show, they were all going to be wonderful.

Anya went out on the open porch area and put some dog food in a bowl near the chair. Soon a familiar figure landed, sampled the food and made himself at home in the chair.

While she was getting ready for work the next morning, she heard barking on her porch, so looked out in time to see the raven hopping up and down on the railing, barking, then dropping pieces of dog food off the deck. When she got downstairs, there were several dogs sitting around under the deck, watching for more treats from the deck.

If her guest was going to be feeding all the strays, she better buy a very large bag of very cheap dog food to keep on hand

Work at the store seemed to free her mind to design more paintings and her breaks and lunch periods were spent sketching out her ideas. At this rate, she would be needing to order more canvases or start painting on wood.

After work, she walked back to the apartment by way of the beach and picked up some interesting driftwood pieces. When she got home with them, she arranged them on the porch, to find which side she liked best and then lightly sketched a raven on one piece. Then she painted in some misty background and started on the raven. She depicted him stashing a shiny trinket into a knothole in the driftwood.

Sandy came up later and when she saw it, she immediately wanted to put it in the shop. Anya wasn't sure she was even done with it and needed to add the glow to the feathers after the undercoat finished drying.

Sandy said these were the best pieces of work she had ever done and she was good, before.

Anya told her she better be careful, she would start believing that and double her prices. Sandy told her she was already planning on at least doubling them, maybe tripling them, these were just that good. But why not wait and see what one brought at auction at the Juneau show?

As she finished a piece, she took it in the apartment to finish drying as she didn't want them to still be wet when packed for the trip to Juneau. Smeary blobs might work for some people as art, but not her.

By the end of the week, she had enough pieces in the works to send a good selection with Sandy. She would continue to work on the ones she had started as she had time.

With Monday being a day off, she had stayed up almost all night working on art

pieces, so she was not to happy when a
couple of hours after she fell asleep, there
came a firm knocking at her door.

When she peeked through the curtain
beside the door, she saw Joel, the town
policeman with a stranger in State Trooper
uniform. She unlatched both locks and the
chain off her door and let them in. She knew
she looked pretty rough but Joel asked if she
was alright and the Trooper looked like he
thought she had been out drinking all night, at
the very least. As they came into her living
room area, the sun came through the clouds
and hit on the paintings she was drying
around the walls.

The feathers on the ravens looked so real
the Trooper almost touched them to see.
Anya suggested he not mess it up unless he
planned on buying it.

"Wow, you painted all of these?" Joel asked
her.

"Yes, these were finished about 2 hours ago.
I worked all night on them."

"So after you worked at the store all day,
you worked all night on these? No wonder
you look a little wrung out."

As she caught a glimpse of herself in a
mirror on the wall, she figured he should have
been a diplomat. The silent Trooper
evidently thought the same thing.

"I'm sorry, Trooper Williams here, flew

over from Juneau this morning and needed to clear up some points about your husband's death and your kidnapping."

"I need some tea before I answer your questions, if you don't mind," she said as she started for the small kitchen in the corner of her living area. "Please, make yourselves comfortable in the living room and I will be only a minute or two."

When she came into the living room a few minutes later with her mug of tea, the two men were still standing but were looking at all of her paintings.

The Trooper started to raise his camera to get some photos of her work and she asked that he not do that as these were not finished or for view yet to the public. She wanted to control their release and have them be fresh at the show in Juneau later this month.

After they were all seated, she asked just what did they need to know?

Joel asked her to go over the whole story again and start at the beginning. Then they could ask for clarification on any points.

So she began when she came home from work and George punched her out. She glossed over stealing food and neglected to mention Philip. Other than that, she told them all she remembered.

Joel thanked her and Trooper Williams said they would be in touch if they needed more information or for her to call him if she thought of anything else.

She told him she had thought and thought about the whole mess and still didn't have a clue what really had happened, just that she was glad to be back and still alive. She would feel even better if all these "accidents" would stop.

After the men left, she fixed another mug of tea and sat down to work on her paintings. She figured she would not be relaxing and getting any more sleep, so might as well work.

Another knock on her door pulled her away from her work, only to realize it was getting dark out and she had worked straight through the day.

When she checked, she saw Sandy standing at the door, so opened it. When Sandy looked around the room, her eyes went wide and she was speechless, which for Sandy was really something.

Chapter 9

The raven started barking on the deck and hopping up and down on the railing, so she and Sandy went out to see what the problem was. Someone was spray painting on the garage and Sandy dropped a pot of flowers from the deck down on him. Her aim was pretty good and the women ran down the stairs and jumped on the person as he staggered upright and knocked him down again. The raven was still hopping up and down and barking, interspersed with chortles so Anya yelled up, "Down Spike, good boy."

Maybe people would think she really did have a dog if she called him Spike. It was as good a name for him as she could think of at the moment. She sat on their prisoner while Sandy called the police and Joel showed up within minutes, in his shirtsleeves and old pickup.

He took some pictures of the words scrawled on the garage after restraining the prisoner and tying him to the bumper for the moment.

Then he helped the women clean the paint off before it got dried on too hard. Paint thinner was one thing Anya had on hand in good supply.

The groggy prisoner started yelling about police brutality and Anya told him to shut up, at least he didn't have to clean up the mess he had made. He said he didn't know anything about it, some guy had paid him to do it as a joke. She just didn't have a good sense of humor. She snarled in his face if he thought a death threat was funny, she could give him something to really laugh about, when Joel dragged her back away from the prisoner.

"Uh, I could get in trouble for letting you actually harm the prisoner. I understand the desire, but since he is in my custody, I am supposed to keep him safe. But his being hired to do this is interesting and I probably would never have heard that, later. He would lawyer up and no info forthcoming. How I am going to get him to jail is going to be interesting."

Anya came out with a length of cord and after they helped get the prisoner into the pickup, she looped the cord around his neck in a hangman's noose and then looped the cord through his wrist restraints and ankles, so if he moved, he would choke himself. He started to jerk away from her as she tied the last knot and gurgled as he pulled the noose tighter.

She loosened it to just snug and told him if

he moved, he would be dead by his own movements before Joel could stop and help him out. Joel gave her an odd look and she told him to just pull the end of the rope and it would all come undone, except the noose so it should help him control the prisoner until he had him inside the jail.

"Hey, my brother was a Scout and I had to learn along with him so he could practice on me."

After Joel left, Sandy and Anya went back up to her apartment. She took some extra treats out to Spike. He was going to be the fattest raven on the island soon. He was certainly a smart bird.

Sandy asked if she was going to be okay. Joel was going to drive by more often, but he was a one man police force on this small island and he could only do so much.

Then they started talking about the upcoming show and both women were bubbling with excitement about the possibilities it represented. They started picking out the works to crate and ship to Juneau. Each artist was limited to 10 works for the Show so it was hard to choose. They soon had the 10 picked out unless they changed their minds. It would take some time to crate each one after she framed them.

She had never had time to really indulge in painting before and she was making the most of it. It certainly kept her mind busy and not dwelling on why someone was trying to kill her and other little things like that.

She fixed a couple of sandwiches for her and Sandy to eat while they looked over the paintings and then decided how to actually crate them. Sandy decided she would drive her van onto the ferry and haul the paintings in the van. That way, they knew how they would be treated all the way and she could cushion them in the back of the van better than normal crates could do.

She knew how hard it could be to find a place to stay in Juneau while government was in session, so figured she could sleep in her van, also.

By the time Sandy left, they had narrowed the selection down to 12 paintings. She thought maybe she would take the extra two just in case. Anya was so tired by this time she locked up the apartment and fell onto her bed and was asleep before she pulled the covers over her..

Foggily, she heard a slight tapping at her back door in the very early morning hours. She woke up enough to realize she was still fully dressed and headed back to see who would be at her back door at this time of day. It wasn't even fully light out.

As she peered through a side window, she recognized Philip and undid the chain and locks to let him in. Today was a work day at the store, so she should thank him for waking her up. She hadn't even set the alarm last night. She started some hot water for tea and he sat at the counter, letting her wake up a bit more. He looked at the paintings he could see from his seat, but did not wander around or indulge in idle chitchat.

As soon as she had her mug of tea and slid one across to him, he smiled at her and told her the way she had trussed up the vandal last night was one of the funniest things he had seen in a long time.

He said he was trying to keep an eye on her and was just about to take the guy when the flower pot hit him, then both of them. He thought it was very entertaining. He did warn her to be extra careful. She told him she still carried his gun and he told her to keep it for the time being. He had another one. He asked for his canister back and she gave it to him.

Then he asked if he could look at her paintings. He was so polite about it that she said sure, if she didn't mind her getting ready for work while he looked.

She went back to brush out her sleep tangled hair and change and he went from painting to painting, but kept going back to the driftwood piece. He asked her how much she was asking for it and she told him she was sending it to the auction and show in Juneau. He told her not to settle for anything less than a number that startled her. He said he really had to be leaving as it was getting almost too light. She let him out the back door and he leaned over and kissed her forehead, telling her she cleaned up nicely. She shut the door, relocking and chaining it in a daze.

She stuffed her lunch in her small pack and headed out the front after giving Spike his breakfast. She always kept the small handgun in her waistband of her jeans, so when she came out the front door, she always had her hand close to the handle of it, under her shirt. By now it was getting to be habit.

Spike chortled to her from the railing and she waved back to him. He really was a good companion, besides being inspiration for her artwork.

When she got home that evening, Sandy had her van pulled up out back and was redoing part of the interior. She tried to use it once a year to take a trip around the southwest Lower 48. She used the ferry system to get to Bellingham, Washington and drove from there.

She was leaving her bed and clothing area but moving the small kitchen out and adding shelves to carry paintings and other art objects for the show. She would have straps fastened on by the time she left, to hold everything in place in case of rough seas.

They had a week left now to get everything loaded and ready for her to go. Anya would keep the gift shop open on her days off and the evenings of the days she worked. Not ideal for Sandy's business, but better than not being open the entire week she would be gone.

The framing looked very good on the paintings that were going. She used driftwood and cut each frame custom to the piece it was to go on. The frames were almost as much a piece of art as the paintings they held, with small embellishments added by hand.

After she saw Sandy off at the dock, she wandered back to the apartment and Spike waddled along with her. He was getting so he ignored most people walking on the sidewalks and tended to take his share out of the middle. He only used the sidewalks when he walked with Anya, so she tried to stay on areas seldom used by others. Not everyone was nice to the friendly raven and she didn't want to have to hurt anyone.

He seemed to have an understanding with the neighborhood dogs, and they kept their distance and he barked at them. He was learning new barks, so sometimes he sounded like a huge guard dog and other times like a yappy lap dog. He seemed to prefer the guard dog sound and used it if anyone came to her door. When he wanted treats, he yapped.

All of the Native people thought she must be okay, since she was friends with Raven. Spike took it all in stride, when they offered him tidbits of fish, he accepted and greedily gulped them down. He really was going to get fat if he didn't watch it.

She opened the gift shop as soon as she finished cleaning up from packing the paintings yesterday, when she got up. There wasn't much to be done in the shop this time of year. She brought some of her art supplies and started painting while tending the shop. Soon a few people were stopping in just to watch her work. Once in a while, they would purchase something while there, so she enjoyed getting to meet more of the town folk and make a little money for Sandy, too.

The night of the auction, Sandy called her and was so excited she could barely speak coherently.

The bidding was going on for the driftwood painting and someone on the phone kept bidding and driving the price sky high. So far it was already the most expensive piece in the whole show and the bidding was still in progress.

Anya hung onto the phone as Sandy gave a bid by bid description. It was like hearing a boxing match on radio. The winning bid was so high Anya about fainted. The phone-in caller was the winning bidder. His card went through, so he had money to back his bidding.

Every piece she had sent, sold. They were the hit of the show and everyone was talking about them. This should jump start her painting career.

Sandy said she would be home on the evening ferry the next day, so not to worry about anything, she had nothing to unpack. She was still excited from the show and auction success.

Anya had trouble falling asleep and couldn't stop thinking about the sale of her paintings. She enjoyed doing them and had always made some spending money selling one here and there when she needed cash, but she had no idea they would sell this well.

Maybe she could buy a pickup. Living on a small island, maybe some kind of boat would be a better idea. She could walk anywhere on land that she needed to go, but it would be nice to leave once in a while, just whenever she felt like it, without having to buy a ticket on either the ferry or a plane.

Chapter 10

Word somehow had spread about her success at the show in Juneau, so at work at the store, several people stopped in just to congratulate her. The attention felt strange and she was happy to have others enjoying her artwork. She usually always did artwork just for her own pleasure and it was nice when others enjoyed it also. Even nicer when they actually liked it well enough to buy it.

She wondered who the mystery buyer was that paid so much for the driftwood painting of Spike stashing a trinket in a knothole. She really liked that picture and hoped whoever bought it would enjoy it as well.

The ferry was late getting in and Anya was already asleep when Sandy got home. Anya opened the gift shop on time and was working on a painting near the front window when Sandy came in a while later. Anya continued painting while they talked about the show and the auction in Juneau. Several people stopped in to see how the painting was progressing and Sandy thought it was a wonderful idea to have her working out where people could watch, if it didn't bother her.

Anya told her nothing seemed to bother her painting and she could talk and share about her work as she proceeded. Sandy asked her if she would be willing to do that in the summer when the tourists came.

Anya asked Sandy what she thought about her buying a small boat. Sandy told her she could buy a fairly good sized one right now, if she wanted to, since the sale. Maybe even the houseboat that was for sale in the harbor. She could move whenever she wanted to and not even have to pack. The owner really wanted to get rid of it and was offering it at a very reasonable price, cheaper than a regular boat.

Wow, she had not ever thought about owning and living on a houseboat. That would take care of several problems all at once. Housing, transportation and plenty of room for her and Spike and her painting.

Sandy knew the owner so called and arranged a meeting at the houseboat for later that afternoon. Anya finally found something she could not paint on through. She was so excited about the houseboat that she finally put her painting materials away and cleaned up the area she was using. Sandy told her to chill a bit as she didn't want to appear too eager to buy.

Sandy closed up the shop and they walked down to the harbor where the houseboat was located. Spike accompanied them and seemed to be energized by being on the docks. A couple of the fishermen were cleaning that day's catch and tossed him various pieces of fish which he caught in midair. Then he barked for more and they thought that was so funny they actually tossed him more.

Shorty was waiting for them on the houseboat and welcomed them aboard. Spike looked him over, hopped up to the roof and balanced, facing into the breeze and held out his wings, so he looked like a masthead.

Shorty walked them through the whole houseboat and explained the way it ran and how much fuel it used. He had just had the bottom redone, so it was good for several more years. His last doctors' report was not favorable to long solitary trips, so he needed to sell and move to a better climate and medical facilities than a small town with a visiting doctor once in a while.

Anya asked if he was okay to take them out for a little run just to see how it did as she had never been on a houseboat before. He was pleased for a chance to go out again on it, so they cast off from the dock and slowly putted out into the open Bay. The houseboat was fairly large and very well set up inside for comfort and ease of maintenance.

They dropped fishing lines over the side

and putted out across the way toward one of the other uninhabited small islands. He showed her how to pick an area to stay and tie off to the trees on land, checking the tide book to make sure she would not be high and dry at low tide.

He suggested that if she did buy it, that she remain at dock in town for the winter and venture out next spring or summer to explore. It could handle the usual conditions around these islands but was not so good in choppy whitecaps that sometimes popped up in winter from a storm.

When they returned to town and docked, she asked how much he wanted for the boat and the figure he named was very reasonable and less than she would have spent on a used small boat or used pickup. She and Sandy looked at each other and slightly nodded. She accepted his price and didn't even haggle over it. He seemed surprised but happy to have made his sale. So they both thought they had a good deal and were happy with it.

She met him the next morning at the bank and they finalized the paperwork and she was the new owner of her home on the water. He told her she could move in any time as he did not have any personal gear on the boat. Then he handed her the keys and wished her the best and to take good care of the boat, it was a lovely home and he already missed it. She told him he could come visit any time he pleased.

Sandy helped her load most of her belongings into the van and hauled it all to the houseboat. The paintings that were finished, she left in Sandy's gift shop to offer for sale. There wasn't much else to move except the old chair that Spike loved. Joel stopped by with his pickup and they soon had it loaded and on it's way to the dock. Spike was upset that it was moved off the deck of the apartment, but when it was placed on the boat, he settled in, chortling and yipping.

He was already a favorite of most of the fishermen on the docks and the peak of the roof on the cabin was his favorite perch to oversee everything happening during the day.

When he perched over the door on the Chief's House on the tiny island in the center of the harbor, she drew his portrait and set up to paint it.

While she worked on deck, under the awning that protected her from weather, several of the fishermen stopped by to watch. One looked familiar but she didn't know who he was. He watched for quite a while, then wandered off, back to his boat and chores, getting ready to fish in the next open period.

She kept the curtains tightly closed so no one could watch in at night from the dock. She did miss having a second story apartment for privacy reasons alone. So she was not expecting any company when she heard a light tapping at her door.

"Who is it?" she asked and heard a low answer, "Philip."

She let him in. No wonder Spike had not made any noise with his approach. He sat down facing the door and asked how she was doing and did she like her new home?

She told him all about it and how she wanted to park it in different areas and paint some different scenes this coming summer. He asked if he could see anything she had on hand, already done. She didn't have anything finished so showed him the one she was working on, of Spike on the Chiefs' House.

As he was leaving, he again kissed her on the forehead. She felt like a little kid he was fond of, when he did that. Spike mumbled a faint sound as he left the boat. Then all was quiet again in her new domain.

Philip started dropping by about once a week, late in the evening and the evenings always ended the same way. A kiss on the forehead. She wondered what he would do if she grabbed him, pulled his face down and kissed him on the mouth.

She sketched out a picture of Philip walking along the beach with Spike waddling along conversing with him. She only showed them both from the back, so no one would recognize the man. Fog was drifting along and it was a misty looking morning. She worked on it some during the evenings and early mornings before work at the store or the gift shop.

Between the two jobs and the money from her paintings, she felt very well off, financially, for the first time ever in her life. So when the fishermen that usually made grocery runs to Seattle during the winter asked if she wanted to place an order, she accepted and spent a couple of evenings pouring over the catalogue for the freeze dried and dehydrated goods they usually hauled up. Everything was in #10 cans, so moisture wouldn't be a problem until she opened a can. Then she would vac pac it into smaller sized portions. She had a lot of storage on the houseboat, so wanted to have plenty on hand just in case she suddenly no longer had either job and her paintings stopped selling.

She had her own generator on board, but while parked here, she hooked into the power outlets and water supply on the dock and paid a monthly fee for the option. There were solar panels on the roof, and a battery bank under the deck, so she could use power from that, in an outage, which happened often to the town generators. She hauled drinking and cooking water on board and kept the potable water tank topped off, too. Her new home was very self contained and she could live quite comfortably on it as long as she liked. When her grocery order came in, the man pulled his boat up next to hers and offloaded right onto her deck. That was perfect and saved a lot of carrying it along the dock. The weather was even nice about it and was not raining or even drizzling a bit.

She managed to get everything put away before the weather changed, then went for an evening stroll along the beach. She still picked up interesting driftwood pieces and was getting quite a stock of them on hand on her rear deck.

Spike continued to bring her shiny pieces of rock and metal on their walks. She placed his treasures in a short bucket she tied to the railing on the boat so he could play in them at his leisure.

Winter was setting in and the days were getting much shorter. The islands in Southeastern Alaska are not as cold or as dark as farther north, but winter is still a time of keeping warm and being careful. A person can die from hypothermia as well as actual freezing and much easier to accomplish due to most folks not thinking about it. But damp chill weather is easy to lose body heat and become disoriented.

The small wood stove in the cabin on the boat kept her living quarters toasty warm and when Philip showed up late one evening, he was showing definite signs of hypothermia. She wrapped him in a warm quilt and made him a cup of very warm tea with honey in it. She prepared a pan of warm water for him to soak his cold feet in and put her warmest hat on his head to stop any further heat loss.

As he sipped the tea and his teeth stopped chattering, he thanked her for rescuing him, yet again. He asked if he could stay and stay out of sight for a few days on her boat. He needed to keep a low profile for a bit.

She asked if he was wanted by the police or if he was doing anything illegal and he said, "No, I am not one of the bad guys no matter how it looks once in a while. I really just need a place to stay and get some strength back."

"Strength back from what?"

"I was snooping where I probably shouldn't have been and got another slight crease, nothing dangerous but it is painful."

She pulled the quilt away and his shirt and saw the blood along his side, yet again. As she washed the wound and applied antiseptic, she counted up the other scars on the part of him she could see. He looked like a lot of people really didn't like him all that much at one time or another.

Under the bullet crease from a few months ago and the spear wound, just before that, there were other, older scars across his body.

None life threatening in and of themselves, but added up, they were quite a collection.

As she traced one with her finger, he grabbed her hand and told her he thought he was going to either go into another line of work or retire, as soon as this job was done.

She heated up some soup for him to drink with his tea, then showed him the spare bedroom. She washed up the few dishes and went to bed, after stoking up the fire.

It was probably dumb, but she believed him. She didn't notice any of the telltale signs of lying when he spoke about his job or anything he was doing. She only hoped she was right and he was one of the good guys. He certainly had not been hanging out with a very good group. She prayed she should not be judging him by the company he kept.

She prepared a filling breakfast before leaving for work. Then made two lunches, one to take with her and one she left in the fridge for Philip. She left a note for him, letting him know where breakfast was and his lunch, without using any names. It looked more like a grocery list.

While working checkout at the store, she thought she saw Trooper Williams from Juneau walking down the street outside, but he was not in uniform, so she wasn't sure.

When she got home, the food was gone that she had prepared and everything was cleaned up, including her breakfast dishes. Hey, maybe it wouldn't be all bad having an invisible room mate.

She prepared an evening meal and tapped on the door of her spare room then placed the tray just inside the door. She and Spike ate out on the deck, since the evening was not too cold yet. She wanted to enjoy her outdoor spare room as long as possible. It reminded her of the deck at the apartment. Partly roofed over and half of it screened so it would be pleasant in the summer.

As she looked it all over, she decided to build some planter boxes to edge the deck with and supply herself with a salad garden during the summer months. No matter where she took the boat in summer, she could enjoy fresh vegetables on a small scale.

Chapter 11

At the gift shop the next day, Sandy loaned her a gardening catalogue and when she saw the temperature controlled opening roofs for small greenhouses, she decided to order some of them and use them for her project on the boat. It would protect the plants from too much wind on the water and open if it got too warm inside. The waterproof liners with a drain hose on them were the next item to catch her eye. She could line her planters using those and have the drain open out over the edge of the deck, so nothing would rot from standing water. She was getting excited to start in on upgrading her home.

By the time Anya went home that evening, she had ordered the clear roof material and operating systems, the liners with hoses and some manufactured lumber substitute that was supposed to last forever, even around salt water, to build her planters out of. She would be checking the freight office daily in a week or two to see if they had arrived yet.

When she saw Joel a few days later, she asked him what had been done with George's remains? She knew she should have asked earlier, but just never seemed to think of it when anyone was handy that might know.

Joel said he didn't know, but would look into it for her. Since they certainly had had enough time to finish whatever they needed to do by now.

Later in the week, he let her know George had been buried in Juneau as at the time, no one knew exactly who he was or if anyone was left to claim him anywhere else. She thanked Joel for finding out. Then asked if she could have a small plaque made, anyway, for him there. No reason to bring him back here, now. Joel said he already told them to do that, pending her decision on moving him or not. He figured it was for the best and she wouldn't have to do anything about it now. She agreed and said it wasn't like they were getting along really well or had any children to remember him, his folks wouldn't want to foot the bill to bring him back home where they lived, either. It was a shame, but no one was going to really miss him. But he did earn that, himself.

She felt bad about his death and the way no one really mourned his passing. After thinking about it, she sent a check to his Mother to help her out a bit, since his Dad was his roll model, and his Mom was too run down to ever leave.

Two weeks later, she regretted it, as his Dad decided she must have money and she should now be supporting them. After all, it is what Georgie would have wanted for them. Anya told Sandy if she pulled anchor and left some fine day, it would be because her ex-in-laws were on their way North to sponge off her.

So in her next letter to them, she asked for the money back as she had unexpected expenses from bills George had run up and just now came due and next of kin for George were expected to pay them. She never heard from them again.

The only way she knew Philip was still around was that the food she prepared daily disappeared and all the dishes were always done when she came home in the evenings from work. She figured it was probably best this way, but she enjoyed talking to him and missed their conversations. Of course, living in the boat harbor, if she were heard talking in the evenings on her boat, people would think she was a bit eccentric and maybe a little crazy.

When she placed his tray of dinner inside his door that evening, she left the door open a bit and asked if he were doing okay? The CD player was going and she kept her voice down so anyone outside could not be sure they were not just hearing the CD player. She had the exterior speaker on low, also, so it should mask almost any sounds from inside the boat.

Philip came over and sat just inside the door and they talked a while. He said he was pretty much healed up now and was feeling very good. He thought he could probably be moving out in a day or so, if she could put up with him that much longer. She said, "What? Lose my dishwasher genie and have to go back to doing them myself? Yes, I would miss that very much indeed."

He told her to be sure and keep her boat in harbor for the next several weeks as it would be dangerous to be out along the small islands for a while. He would not explain, but she figured it had to do with the drug labs on the small islands dotting the Inside Passage. Possibly some being arranged going up the large Stikine River on the mainland. The river is so large and the volume of water so fast that it is possible to dip fresh water from the visible river stream out in the ocean a long ways from the mouth of the river.

She had not been up the river itself, but had been in a small boat when they went over the river out in the main ocean channel between islands. The river water was raised above the ocean level and a different color. It looked very odd.

Anya figured if anyone wanted to know what was going on out in the woods or up the river, they should just hang out in one of the many bars in town. Even though the population was small, there were very few actual secrets. Someone, somewhere would have noticed increased activity, even if it were only more boat traffic or aircraft of one sort or another. Those made noise and someone would always comment on it to someone else.

Philip said he always tried to be in one of the bars along the docks late in the evenings when he was out and about. He heard the best info then, just before closing.

While they were talking, there was a light tapping at her door. She pulled the door almost shut and went to see who would be at her home this time of night. The person outside was very tall and without a light on her deck, she could not see who it was.

"Who is it?"

"Officer Williams, Ma'am."

She opened the door a crack but it was still on the chain and she had the handgun in her other hand, "Yes? What can I do for you?"

"Um, may I come in? I feel like I have a target on my back standing here in the doorway."

She closed the door and unhooked the chain, then reopened the door. He slipped inside quietly and she pointed out a chair in the dim interior light. The only bright light was over her painting she had been working on earlier.

"Ma'am, I need to find a fellow named Philip Buldock."

"Who is he?"

He slumped down a little in his seat and told her he was hoping she would know how to get in touch as he had some important information that Philip needed.

She told him she really didn't know anyone named that although it was possible he did live on the island as a couple of other people had mentioned the name to her in the last few weeks. Was he wanted for something?

He said he couldn't discuss anything with her and she said in that case, he might as well go. As he went out the door, he turned back and told her if she ever did see Philip, to let him know that he really needed to get in touch with him. She asked what Philip looked like. He just threw up his hands and left.

Philip told her good job, when she went passed his door on her way to bed that night.

He was gone when she got up the next morning. He left a printed note that looked like her grocery list to let her know he was gone. Nothing was spelled out but she got the idea.

Even though they never really spent time together while he stayed with her, she missed him when he was gone.

Her planter supplies finally came in and she

was having fun designing her new planting areas. Spike supervised and she constructed. He tended to play in the screws since they were bright and shiny, so she had to keep them closed in their box. Then he learned how to open the box.

Even though it took twice as long to finish her planter boxes, with Spike's "Help", she was also entertained by his antics and laughed so much she ached. When she fastened the clear tops on the boxes, they fit perfectly and she was amazed. Now all she needed to do was find some good potting soil to fill them with.

Before she put the liners in the boxes and the hoses out the drain holes, she ran a heat cable around the bottom of the box and put the plug-in so she could use her generator power or the city power she was now on.

She planned on trying to grow salad greens most of the winter. Maybe some kale and swiss chard, also. Green vegetables were hard to find in winter here. The seeds she ordered had arrived also, so she could plant as soon as she filled the planters with soil.

She asked one of the fishermen from one of the boats near hers, to save some of the fish waste for her to use as fertilizer under her plants. He said he would, then she went looking for seaweed and small gravel to put in the bottom of the planter first.

She knew there were a few bags of potting soil left in the storeroom at the store she worked at, so she asked the manager the next morning about buying it.

He was more than happy to get it out of the way for the winter and even made a good price if she would take it all. She asked if he would deliver it, since she no longer had a vehicle and he said he would be happy to.

After the potting soil was delivered, Spike made a pest of himself by opening every single bag to see what was in it and then grumbled because each one was just dirt. Then she had to hurry up and fill the boxes, first with the gravel, then seaweed and finally the bucket of fish guts delivered to her by the fisherman. Anya hurried to dump and cover to keep Spike from gorging on them. As it was, he was front heavy for a while after she finished. Once she had all the soil in the planters that she needed, she had to rebag and hide the bags in the store room to keep Spike from opening each of them yet again. Working with Spike could be a challenge.

Chapter 12

Trooper Williams showed up at the store, next, asking her about Philip Buldock. She asked him if he had a photo so she could see what this man looked like so she could tell him if she had ever seen the man. He left in a huff.

He came back a few hours later with several photos and asked her if she recognized any of the men. As she looked through them, there was indeed a photo that might have been Philip but she didn't think so, and one of the men seen later, but the only one she could point out was the man she saw shoot Philip with the spear gun and then get shot himself. She pointed that photo out to Trooper Williams and said he was the only one that she sort of recognized.

He was disappointed in her selection and kept asking if she were sure. She finally told him she did not know any of the other people and for all she knew, they could all be upstanding citizens added to make a line-up. He grumbled but put the photos away. She really didn't know what he wanted her to say.

She asked him if he just wanted her to randomly pick out someone and say that's him? He said No, but he still thought she was not telling him the truth. Then she got mad.

"So basically, you think I am a liar and am holding out some sort of evidence on you? That is sure nice to know you have such a good ability to read my mind when I don't even know what you are wanting. If you want to talk to me again, bring Joel with you and good day, Officer Williams."

She stomped back to the break room and slammed the door shut. That man certainly knew how to rub her the wrong way. She just could not like him and neither did Spike.

The manager came back a few minutes later and asked what the problem was. She said she didn't have a problem but the Trooper sure did. The manager told her that Trooper was considered very good at his job and had a high success rate bringing in criminals. She asked how he did it, by accusing them and browbeating them until the confessed whether they did it or not?

He stopped and looked at her and said that was strange, several people he had arrested said the same thing about him. She asked if his success rate also included confirmed guilty verdicts or just arrests? Very few actual guilty verdicts were credited to him.

When she got home, there was a notice on her door about excess noise after 8 pm in the evenings. She walked back to City Hall and asked about that. They did not know what it was about as the City noise ordinance was for 10 pm and no complaint had been filed against her.

The next evening, another notice was for keeping a public nuisance (Spike) on the premises. Again, she walked to City Hall and asked about it. The Clerk was upset and said she would ask around unofficially and see just what was up. Everyone liked Spike.

The next notice was for lewd behavior and was her final straw. She went from boat to boat, asking everyone still around if anyone had seen anyone around her boat and showed the notices around for all to see. The only person seen on the docks that did not belong was Trooper Williams.

She took the notice to City Hall again and talked to the Clerk about what she had been told. Carmen was really upset and called Juneau to talk to her counterpart there. Everyone thinks the Mayor and Council runs the town, but it is really the Clerks that have the power and know who to talk to, to get things done.

The Clerk in Juneau called back within a few minutes and told Carmen that Trooper Williams was on suspension for suspected activities but could not say at present what those activities were. So Carmen told her what was happening here and started getting the word around on his behavior. She told Anya not to worry and if there were ever any notices from the town, it would be handed to her by Joel, not left tacked to her door on the boat where the weather could remove or ruin it before she got it.

As she was walking down the dock toward her boat, she heard Spike barking. She saw someone jump to the dock from her boat and yelled "Hey."

Several people on other boats looked to see what she was yelling about, so she continued yelling, "Hey you, what were you doing on my boat?"

The man took off running and someone 'happened' to pull a rope taut across the dock as the man ran by, tripping him very well, then several of the fellows jumped forward to 'help' him up and managed to manhandle him quite well. It was Trooper Williams, out of uniform and several of the local men had good reason to 'help' him rather roughly.

Someone called Joel and he showed up while they still had a good hold of Trooper Williams. Carmen had already called him to fill him in on the notices posted on Anya's boat, so he already had a good head of steam as he came down the dock.

Everyone headed back to Anya's boat and she went on board to see what he had been doing this time. He sputtered that the vandalism was already done when he got there and he was just gathering evidence. No one believed him, especially after the pseudo notices he had been leaving on Anya's door and the dirt from her planters all over his boots and hands.

Her planters were emptied of dirt and it with the fish guts and seaweed were scattered all over her deck. An oily rag was stuffed in the air intake on her motor. Random obscenities were scrawled on her windows. The crowd was starting to turn ugly and told Joel if he would let them have the guy a while, he would at least clean up the mess he had made. Joel said he was sorry, but he couldn't do that, but he would be back to help clean it all up.

Williams was cursing and threatening everyone that had helped catch him and especially Anya for being an unmentionable word she only knew from reading books. Jerry, one of the local boat owners was catching the whole thing on video, so there would be no weaseling out later and saying he never said any of those things. Even better was the fact that Joel had read him his Rights at the start and he still continued spouting off.

After Joel and Williams left, Spike came

chirruping down from where he had stayed all through the commotion, high on a mast of one of the fishing boats. She sat on the side of the deck, just looking at the ruin of her deck. Soon people started showing up. Two had large brooms and swept up most of the dirt and assorted fish parts to put back in the planter boxes. Then they scrubbed down the deck to remove any lingering traces and a couple more helped on cleaning up the windows. They told her she should not have to see what had been written there. Joel had taken pictures earlier to use as evidence.

Anya was wondering just why he was targeting her when someone mentioned she looked a lot like his soon to be ex-wife. He was always a little tightly wound, but now the strings had snapped.

The light tapping on her door didn't even surprise her, later that night. Philip slipped in and asked her how she was. She told him the whole thing and asked why Williams was so intent on getting him? Philip told her Williams blamed him for his marriage breaking up. He didn't even know William's wife, but that little fact didn't matter to Williams. He witnessed Williams hit his wife on a street in Juneau and grabbed Williams while his wife got away. That was the only time he ever saw the woman. She never went back to Williams and filed for divorce.

Anya fixed them some tea and sandwiches and they sat in silence, sipping tea and eating the sandwiches. She would replant her boxes tomorrow and wondered if any of the first seeds planted would manage to come up, also. It would make her plant boxes varied and interesting. He said it was good that she could look at the brighter side, anyway. She said any other way of looking at it didn't make it any better, so might as well look on the bright side.

After Philip left, she locked up for the night. She considered getting an actual dog, although Spike did a fair job at warning of intruders. He wasn't one to keep in the house, though. Plus he did tend to roam once in a while.

When she got up, Spike was chortling on deck and there was some boxes with already started plants for her boxes in them. There were only a couple of people on the island that had gardens, but someone had shared some of their hard work. She looked all over for a note, but found none. She didn't even know who to thank for such a thoughtful gesture.

After she planted the plants and watered them in, she left for work at the gift shop. She talked to Sandy about who could possibly have given her such a thoughtful gift. Sandy had a few ideas, but nothing definite.

As she painted in front of the main window that afternoon, several people stopped in to tell her how sorry they were that she had been having such a time on their island. That it really was a nice little place and everyone was hoping she would stay. Even most of the ones considered soreheads were being nice to her. Sandy thought it was almost scary but in a nice way.

There was a bucket of fresh caught shrimp on her deck when she got home. Spike was trying to figure out how to open the lid, but so far had not managed it. She immediately prepared a large pan of shrimp scampi and soon a few neighbors followed their noses over to see how she was doing. She invited them to stay for dinner as she had plenty and would still have leftovers. Someone brought garlic bread and someone else had a nice salad and soon it was a feast.

Spike pigged out on the scraps when she cleaned the shrimp, so he was quiet all through dinner. He sat on top the roof peak and kept lookout, chortling once in a while to make his views known.

Chapter 13

Her small fridge had a very small freezer, so she had shrimp for dinner for a couple of days, even making beer batter, and deep frying some one evening. Someone brought over a 'chicken' halibut and she added strips of it to the batter and fried them up for a seafood platter. Then one night there was seafood chowder that was a big hit with everyone on the dock.

She liked to cook and they liked to eat, so it worked out quite well, with them supplying the seafood.

Her little mini-greenhouse planters were doing quite well after she added some grow lights in them. The heat cables under the soil and the light from the lamps made them produce very well for fresh salads with her meals. All the fish fertilizer she was adding to the boxes had to help, also.

Two or three of the men started stopping by almost every evening, and two seemed to think she should pick one of them to be her steady guy. She wasn't even used to being a widow, let alone think about starting another relationship. One told her he understood, but wanted her to be thinking about it. The other one, Randy, took it as rejection and was starting to get obnoxious about it. Spike was taking delight in yapping at him like a small yappy dog.

When she saw him swing at Spike, she lit into him and told him he was no longer welcome to come around at all. She already experienced one abusive relationship, she was not now or ever going to even consider another one.

He got all huffy and said taking a swing at a stupid bird was certainly not a reason to think he would ever treat her that way. She told him it didn't matter, she was not going to chance it and find out the hard way he wouldn't control his temper. Usually tempermental meant far more temper than mental.

He started showing up at odd times throughout the day at the store, then he started dropping in at the gift shop, just standing there, watching her paint. He was getting on her nerves and creeping her out, with his behavior.

She was talking to the owner of the boat he worked on, one day in the store when Randy stormed in, ranting that she was trying to get him fired. The boat owner looked at him in amazement and asked him what he was talking about. He started sputtering about her having it in for him and trying to get him fired. The boat owner said, "Not that it is any of your business just what we were talking about, but she was asking me to bring her some rock fish on our next trip out, if we got any incidental in our nets when we pulled them."

Randy had the grace to sputter out an apology before backing away and leaving the store. Earl turned back to her and asked just what that was all about.

She didn't want to cause Randy any more problems than he was causing himself, but after that little outburst, she figured she should still stick to telling the truth and told Earl all about how Randy was harassing her and practically becoming a stalker.

Earl said he might be able to help a bit, on that. He may just go ahead and fire Randy the next time they were on some other island. He was not a good worker and always blamed someone else for his shortcomings. He was getting tired of ruffled crew feathers all the time, it gave a man an ulcer.

Earl's boat was starting to pull away from the dock, the next morning, when Randy came running down the steps and jumped on board. Earl jumped on him for being late and everyone else having to load the supplies without his help. He blamed the motel for not waking him up early enough and they were underway. Anya was glad to see them go and have a respite, at least until they returned home.

When The Happy Lady returned to dock later in the week, Randy was not aboard. One of the crew members had a bandaged hand, the other one told her later that Randy was saying some really obnoxious things about her and the crew sort of thought of her as their little sister that knew how to cook and no one was going to bad mouth anyone that could make chowder and biscuits like hers. By the way, did she have any leftover cake getting old? Oh yeah, Randy got dropped off near Juneau. Let him irritate the Legislature.

She figured that was worth a new cake, so she made one that evening and delivered it to The Happy Lady.

The approaching Christmas season is always reason to be happy, and this year, Anya planned on making sure many others had a nice Christmas, too. There weren't many homeless or truly underprivileged folks on the island, but she wanted to have a celebration that everyone could join in.

She started by talking to Carmen. That woman was a storehouse of knowledge about everyone that lived there. She knew which ones would be upset if they thought someone was offering charity.

They decided to make it a community

dinner and gift sharing. No one had to bring gifts, there would be gifts under a large tree to be handed out after the dinner. Dinner could be buffet style so everyone could pick and choose what they actually liked.

Carmen contacted the fishing boat that usually made the run to Seattle for groceries to sell at the docks and arranged for him to purchase enough for a feast for the whole town and a list of items to purchase for gifts. Anya used part of the commissions she received on her latest group of paintings to be sold to pay for everything.

Carmen informed the Mayor that they were having the Christmas party at the Community Center on Christmas Eve. He wanted to change the name to Holiday Celebration and both Carmen and Anya vetoed that. He could be as politically correct as he wanted on his own money and time, they were doing this, they would call it what they wanted. He caved.

They put up posters at the Post Office and left flyers at all the bars. Most businesses around town let them add posters in the front windows. One was placed on the steps going down to the docks, even. Everyone on the island would know about it by Christmas.

Philip came by one morning as she was heading to the gift shop. He asked if she could take the day off and come with him and a friend to pick out a tree, over on the mainland where the choices might be better. They walked on to see Sandy and she asked if it would be okay. Sandy asked if there was room for one more and closed up shop for the day to go also.

Carmen said the Community Center could handle a 12 foot tree easily, so they were going to look for one.

Philips friend had a nice small fishing boat and they were soon on their way. The men had decided the best trees would probably be up the Stikine River a ways, so they headed over to check it out.

After several hours of not finding the perfect tree, they decided maybe they were not ever going to agree on what made a perfect tree. With millions of acres of forest all around them, something was always wrong. They finally picked one that was almost perfect and another to use the extra limbs to fill out the other and have limbs to use for decorations. They cut cedar boughs to add a lovely odor to the Hall.

By the time they got the tree set up, they were all laughing. School was out for Christmas so they had announced that anyone wanting to help decorate the tree would be welcome. Frazzled mothers dropped off their children, hoping to get last minute shopping done, not that there was a lot of choices for shopping. If things were not ordered ahead of time so it would arrive in time, people did without.

Anya let out an ear splitting whistle and soon it was very quiet in the Hall. The kids were looking with interest to see how she did it. So she showed them and then set each small group to certain tasks. She told them there would be small prizes throughout the day for different chores. She had boxes full of the very coolest hats and mitts that could be found in Seattle this late in the winter. She had made sure there would be enough so each child would end up with at least a set. Several of the sets included scarves. She really wished she had been able to figure out a way to do boots and coats, too. Several of the children needed them.

There was a table with sandwiches and fruit on it for anyone wanting something to eat. The bottles of juice were in tubs of ice, and then there was hot chocolate available in pump pots so it would not be too hot.

The groups were busily making sparkling paper chains, cutting out snowflakes and making garlands and wreathes. They would only be using handmade ornaments except the small lights the men had wound around the tree before standing it up and the large star on top fastened to the lights. They rightly figured that would be difficult to do once the tree was up. Getting any ornaments to the top would be a challenge, anyway.

By the time the piles of chains and snowflakes were threatening to overflow the Hall, they started winding them around the tree and hanging the snowflakes. Most were made of the prettiest sparkling paper she could find. Then glue sticks and glitter did the rest. Each child's pile of ornaments was judged the best for one reason or another and each could choose a set of mitts and hat and a scarf if it came with one.

When the children were picked up later in the day, she asked the parents if they could help her out as she had too many sets and didn't know what to do with them. Since it was the truth, most parents had no trouble picking out a set or two for children at home.

She was well pleased that most sets were gone by the end of the day. She was not prepared for the Scrooge factor when Randy came in through the door as she was getting ready to leave. She did not think he was coming in to add joy to the preparations for a happy celebration.

Chapter 14

As she backed away from the door, he advanced toward her. He was so intend on whatever he had planned that he did not see Sandy and Philip over behind the tree, putting away the last of the lunch supplies.

"So, Randy, what a surprise to see you here. I thought you were happy in Juneau."

"I had unfinished business here, you got me fired."

"No, Randy, I did not get you fired. You got yourself fired. No Captain is going to allow someone to disrupt his crew and start fights while on board and working."

She had raised her voice enough that Philip and Sandy both were now headed her direction but were behind Randy so he did not see them. He grabbed her shirt front and was dragging her toward him when Sandy smacked him over the head with the large stainless steel thermos she brought hot chocolate in.

Philip grabbed him before he hit the floor and was dragging him out the door before Anya even knew what had just happened. One minute she is being dragged forward by a stalker and the next, he is being dragged out the door. If looks did not deceive her, he was unconscious. Philip dragged him right on down to the town jail and was only inside a few minutes before stepping back out to see if she wanted to come in and swear out a complaint against him.

She really didn't want to, but he was now becoming physically intimidating and maybe dangerous to her. Sandy walked in the station with her and Joel was just coming back from the back room that they used as a jail.

Joel asked how they knocked him out and Sandy spoke up and told him about her thermos she was still carrying. He hefted the thermos and said it was as good as a large rock and Randy was still out, would probably have a king sized headache tomorrow.

Anya told him what was said and how Randy had grabbed her by the shirt and was dragging her out when Sandy hit him. Who knows just what he may have done if he had managed to get her outside away from people.

They found a ratty old van parked a short ways from the Community Center, and when Joel called it in, it was registered to Randy and he had came back to town on the ferry that evening, from Juneau. Joel opened the door and there was duct tape and assorted knives and rope in the back of the van. All the seats were gone and the windows painted black on the inside. It did not look like she would have enjoyed a ride in that van, at all. Philip suggested to Joel that he check around the rest of the State and maybe even Outside to see if any possible links to stalking or serial killings would match.

Anya was still shaken up quite a bit, so she went over to Sandy's and Philip accompanied them. They stopped on the way and picked up a pizza to share. Later, after they all relaxed a bit, Philip walked her home to her boat. Spike was nestled into his chair on deck and muttered at them as they came on board, but did not get up.

Tomorrow would be a very long day, getting the meal prepared for the entire community. So Philip did not stay long after checking to make sure Randy didn't have an accomplice hiding out here in wait for Anya. He didn't want to say anything in case she had not thought of it herself. He didn't want to scare her too much, but she could still be in danger.

She actually had thought of it but didn't want to say anything and have Philip think she was jumping at shadows. She kept the handgun under her pillow at night so it would be handy. During the day, she usually had it in her waistband or a handy pocket. She figured she would rather be safe than sorry that she left it home. She had broken her own rule today since she was going to be working with children all day. She should have known better and just carried it.

She was up and ready to go very early, so walked on down to the Community Center to get started on the day's cooking. She could prepare jelled molds and pies now in the industrial kitchen in the Hall and have things prepped for the main cooking later.

By the time the first people that had volunteered to help started showing up, she had the molded salads made and in the walk-in fridge and the relish trays prepped, wrapped and in the fridge, also. She was in the middle of peeling mounds of potatoes. A couple of people took over peeling so she started making cream fillings for the pie shells lined up along the counters. The filled pies were cooling to place in the walk-in.

Bread dough was raising to make dinner rolls later. The first turkeys would be coming out of the ovens very soon and the next ones put in. The turkeys would be sliced after they cooled a bit, then put on covered platters to reheat as they were needed to serve. Some broth poured over the slices before covering the platters would assure moist slices instead of dried out slices being served.

They were well ahead of schedule when the first people started showing up for dinner. There were relish trays set around the hall with other trays of cheese and crackers to nibble on while waiting. Pitchers of fruit punch were set around on all the tables and small glasses nearby for anyone needing something to drink. The Community Center looked beautiful with the giant tree decorated by the children the day before lighted and glowing splendidly.

The evening progressed beautifully. The bartender from the roughest bar in town, had a lovely full white beard and played Santa to the hilt, no padding necessary. The hardest part of the evening for him was keeping his language Santa-like. He found that he was a natural with the kids and they all sat around while he told fishing stories after the gifts had been handed out and the parents relaxed before everyone went home.

As the meat was carved from the turkeys during the day, Anya started huge stock pots full of soup simmering. The trimmings from assorted vegetables were added along the way and there would be enough to feed the whole community another meal, if they wanted to do this again, as a get-together evening. What was planned for New Years day?

She asked everyone if they wanted to come back for a soup and sandwich evening on New Years Day and everyone did. She would freeze the soup and finish it on the day of the next get-together.

By the time she was able to leave, she was

very tired and not paying attention as well as she should have, so she was doubly thankful that Philip was still lingering to walk her home when 2 men walked back into the kitchen and started to drag her out the back door. She shrieked loud enough to wake all the dogs in town and pulled the handgun from her pocket and started shooting. Her accuracy wasn't great, since one had her arm and she shot him in the foot. The other one grabbed for her and she shot him in the arm. Then she threw up.

Philip came through the door at a run and stopped in amazement. She was leaned over throwing up and still holding her gun on the two men she had just shot. Technically, it was his gun, but he now considered it hers, since she had it longer than he had.

The one holding his arm was moaning about Randy wasn't paying them enough for this and the other one was trying to shush him. He said a joke is one thing but getting shot was not a joke and he wasn't going to be part of anything involving guns. This was not his idea of a fun way to spend Christmas Eve.

When Philip told him he would be spending it in jail, he was even less happy. When they got to the jail and he found that Randy had the cell next to him, he got very verbal even after Joel read him his Rights.

Since there was not a regular doctor on the

island, and no traveling doctor was available at the present, the nurse practitioner and Joel would be the ones tending the gunshot wounds.

All the time the pair were working on the one that was complaining the most, he was yelling at Randy about lying to him and trying to pass this off as a surprise elopement with his girlfriend. Then he turned on his partner in crime and told him he knew he was as dumb as a box of rocks, why didn't he stop them before they got to this fix?

His partner just said he really needed the money and it seemed okay at the time. Neither man was willing to remain silent and take the blame for what they had thought was a harmless prank that paid well.

Anya wondered what they were intending to do, since Randy was locked up, if they had made it out the door with her. Joel asked him that and he looked dumbfounded a minute. "I never even thought of that. Hey, Billy, what WERE we going to do with her after we got outside, since the guy that hired us is in jail?"

Billy was not inclined to answer, but he did appear to be thinking it over. Then he did answer and told them she was supposed to be held in an old fishing shack down the coast a ways and that Randy fully expected to be out of here in a couple of days. Some technicality or other. He said he had a very good lawyer.

Joel called Juneau and asked to have the Troopers come and transfer his prisoners to the Juneau facility as they had more room and 2 of his inmates were injured. They were not thrilled to be transferring prisoners on Christmas.

Joel walked with Philip and Anya toward the docks while they discussed the evening's planned and unplanned events. When they were a few blocks from the jail, they heard a shot that sounded like a high powered rifle. All three immediately hit the deck and stayed down. No further gunfire sounded, so after a few minutes, they returned to the jail.

Only one shot had been fired and that was all that was needed by the shooter to take care of the problem of Randy. He had been shot through the head from somewhere across the street on one of the business roofs that looked directly down into the jail.

The jail windows were only safety glass with wire in them, not bulletproof. Usually the only inmates were drunks sleeping it off or someone picking a fight. Kidnapping was unheard of for this small town, no place for anyone to go with the kidnapped victim unless they had a boat or plane.

Joel called Juneau back and told them the main problem inmate had just been murdered, so no rush on picking up the other two. He offered to let one of the prisoners have the now vacant cell, but neither one wanted it and preferred staying in the one they were sharing.

Jerry and Billy both were more talkative without Randy in the next cell. They said he was the person everyone went to for drugs, when you were pulling line or nets in the middle of a fishing open and the fish were running and money to be made but no time for sleep. He could supply pills to stay awake and pills to sleep, then more to wake you up again. He was a walking pharmacy.

Randy had been talking about some new stuff he would be handling soon. Maybe his supplier didn't want him cutting a deal with whatever information he might have. The woman was just his private vendetta.

Joel decided he better look that van over a lot closer, when it got daylight or pull it into a lighted garage to really search and tear it apart.

Joel asked Philip some questions, then deputized him to help him out since the little town seemed to be having a crime spree of sorts. He was getting sleep deprived.

They walked Anya home and checked out her houseboat before leaving. She wasn't feeling too sleepy, so stayed up a while, trying to piece together what was happening around this quiet little town.

A few days later, she awoke to the sound of Spike, barking his intruder alarm. When she went to the door, there was a stranger standing there. She stepped out to see what he wanted. The man was staring at Spike, fascinated by the barking raven hopping around on the roof over the deck. Several crew members on the closest boats were watching to see if she was okay.

The stranger offered her his card, Ruben Jones - art buyer. She looked up at him in surprise. He told her that Sandy had sent him on over, after he stopped in at the gift shop. While they were still standing on the deck, talking, Sandy came trotting down the dock.

"Hi, sorry I am late. I wanted you to meet Mr. Jones and planned on getting here before he did, but a customer showed up just as I was locking up. I swear they take longer when they see you are in a hurry to leave."

Anya invited them inside and Spike quit barking. The painting she had been working on was still set up in the living room and others were drying around the room. It was not warm enough to paint on deck any more.

Mr. Jones went from painting to painting and finally stood in front of the one she was working on. He asked her if she had an agent. She pointed to Sandy.

"No, I mean a real agent, someone to

represent you in New York or just Seattle, even."

"No, I have not had a need for an agent."

"Well, you really do need one to negotiate better terms for you for your work and to represent you to Galleries in the large cities."

"Why would I need to hire someone and pay a wage for all of that when I am selling everything I can paint right here and Sandy actually pays me for doing it, not me paying her?"

"But you could travel, live anywhere you like."

"I like right where I am living, my friends are all here and I own my home and can park it anywhere I feel like staying for as long as I want to stay."

He seemed stumped by her answer. Didn't all women want to live in New York and have unlimited shopping? His wife certainly did and would kill him if he suggested she come see how this artist lived, not even suggest that she actually try it.

Sandy brought up that one of the pictures was a scene Anya remembered from when she was kidnapped and made her escape across the islands on foot. Mr. Jones was flabbergasted, this young woman had saved herself, then walked back to town? Taking several weeks to manage it and living off the land? Unbelievable. She would be an instant hit on the talk show circuit and her paintings would become all the thing to own. She could become very rich indeed.

He dangled these little jewels of luxury in front of her and she turned it all down. He finally was rendered speechless. She must be an idiot savant, able to paint brilliantly and no sense other than that. He just could not understand someone turning down the wonderful life style he was laying out in front of her and she was trampling all over it.

By the time he left, he was a sadly disillusioned man. He had been so positive he was the bearer of glad tidings and a wonderful way of life to a poor misguided woman living in the wilds of Alaska, for heavens sakes. Nobody lived in Alaska on purpose, did they?

Chapter 15

After Mr. Jones left, Sandy and Anya sat out on the deck, eating sandwiches and feeding Spike. Sandy asked her if she was sure she wasn't interested in New York and the city life.

She laughed and said it would drive her nuts within 24 hours. She hated the one time she had spent a week in Seattle. George had been adamant about their staying the full week, but finally gave in and they came home 2 days earlier than originally planned. Seattle would seem like a village compared to New York City.

"I was hoping you would stay, but I didn't want to influence your decision in any way, so let him try to convince you without saying anything one way or another."

Anya continued to work her 3 days a week at the store and 3 days a week at the gift shop. She figured if she quit work and only painted, she might get tired of it after a while and preferred to keep it something she loved to do and had to find time for.

The turkey soup and sandwich feast was a hit for New Years Day. Some people had hangovers and not in too festive a mood, but they all showed up anyway. She added homemade noodles to the soup and it was hot, filling and delicious. At least the new year was going great. No one had tried to kidnap or kill her so far.

Her houseboat was proving to have been an excellent investment. It was economical on heating fuel and the utilities were very reasonable. She had plenty of room and it was easy to keep looking great. She sketched then painted a portrait of Spike on the front of the cabin. He would sit and watch her paint it, then stand and admire himself in the painting.

Several of the other boat owners asked about paintings for their boats, too. She hated to turn them down, but asked them to check out her work at the gift shop and see what they wanted to spend on boat art.

When she awoke, the world was so still and white, she didn't know what happened until she stepped out and saw all the snow. She hurried dressing and started shoveling off her deck. She did not want to be one of the boats that sunk each year from lack of keeping the snow shoveled off. When she was through with her deck, she started shoveling off the dock and floating stairs. At the top of the stairs, she looked at town and it looked so lovely and clean. She hurried back and got her camera to take some pictures. Southeastern Alaska doesn't get a lot of snow in winter and it is always lovely. Then she snapped some pictures of Spike cleaning his feathers with snow in a rowdy snow bath.

She was more than ready for a hot chocolate break by the time she went indoors. Her boots and clothes were soggy from the wet snow and a quick hot shower felt wonderful while the water heated for the chocolate. When she checked the time, she added some soup and had lunch.

She spent the afternoon sketching out some pictures of Spike playing in the snow. He was having so much fun, he was just like a kid. Soon he was shivering. She set her small electric heater by the porch door and left the door open a little bit. When he found the heat, he plopped down right in front of it and kept turning like he was on a rotisserie.

Anya figured Spike was a young bird and maybe his parents were killed or died and he latched onto her as a source of food. He didn't seem to have many skills at searching out any other source of food and came to her whenever he was hungry. He would follow her around with his mouth wide open, begging. She didn't think his behavior was like the usual wild bird. She was glad of his company, and happy to have him around.

There was more snow the next morning, so

she again shoveled off her boat and the dock and stairs. Several of the other boat owners were gone on vacation or if they lived in the off season in other States, had gone home. She wasn't sure what the snow load was, but this was wet heavy snow and she was getting worried about a couple of the boats at the end of the dock that seemed to be riding a lot lower in the water than before.

By the end of the week with constant additional snow, she was really getting worried about those boats. She asked Sandy what should be done. Sandy suggested asking the Harbor Master and see what he had to say.

The Harbor Master said he had notified all the owners but two and now it was up to them whether or not they wanted to hire someone local to go on board and clear the snow or take their chances on the boats sinking if the weather didn't clear. No one should go on any of the boats without permission, so leave them alone. He said the two he could not get in touch with were not usual winter time customers here, and he had not seen them before they left. It was their two boats riding the lowest in the water.

Now that she had his curiosity aroused, he decided they should go check them out and if needed, go ahead and clear the boats to save them. They walked down the stairs to the floating dock and clear to the end of the dock where the two boats were moored. There were some empty spaces between those two boats and the others wintering over, and no prints in the snow leading to the boats, but a lot of bird activity around the vents from below and the passageway leading down.

As they got closer to the boat, there was an unpleasant odor. The Harbor Master decided they would have Joel check out the boat with them, so went back and called him in.

When Joel got there, he didn't really want to go aboard and check it out, either and wondered if maybe they should call the troopers in from Juneau. They decided if it was just a hold with rotted fish left in it, they would look pretty silly, so went on board.

Joel was complaining a little bit about only taking this job because it was supposed to be to keep the drunks from becoming a public nuisance and keeping the different boat crews from causing too much trouble when they wanted to celebrate and each one blamed the others for some imagined slight. He didn't really have police experience and there had been too much violence involving guns and knives lately, for his peace of mind.

When he opened the door leading below decks, he about threw up. The smell was horrific. The sight of the captain and two man crew on top of a partly full hold of rotting fish didn't help his stomach, either.

They had obviously all been there for quite some time.

"Okay, I'm calling Juneau. They can come take care of this."

The sister boat across the dock had the same odor, so they did not even go on board. When the two Troopers showed up a few hours later, they shooed everyone back from the smelly boats and then decided it might be better to dry dock the boats and check them out on land. No evidence would be lost into the ocean, this way.

The full team would be arriving soon from Juneau to process the boats and contents. They would just guard the site.

Anya went home. She did not want to see whatever they found, although she already knew it would not be pretty. Joel was still a little green around the edges from his brief glimpse in the hold, she didn't have to ask for details.

She fixed him some peppermint tea and a plate of crackers to help settle his stomach. The Harbor Master joined them and was happy to be away from the two boats.

Philip came by and stopped at her boat to see what was going on. All four sat around and discussed possibilities of what could have happened at the two boats. None of their theories were very good and she hoped they were all wrong and the fellows were overcome by fumes form old fish and just passed out to die from exposure or whatever, no one else involved at all.

As the first boat was lifted and swung over into dry dock, a muffled boom sounded inside, followed by another, louder explosion. Evidence rained down all over the place and anyone even slightly close was going to be trying to get the smell off for days afterwards.

The second boat was treated with kid gloves and an explosive device was located just inside the door leading to the hold. If Joel had taken one more step, he would now be mixed in the mess scattered all over the dock and bank of the little harbor. He was very glad to have a delicate stomach after thinking about that for a while.

A second device was on a delayed timer attached to the first device and set to go within seconds of the first one being tripped.

As they removed the captain and crew, they found some boxes under only a few rotted fish that would have covered them completely before the fish rotted almost away. When the boxes were opened, they contained a large assortment of street drugs and pot.

Philip said it looked like the captain and crew had gotten stupid and tried holding out product from the people they were delivering for. Never a good idea at any time. Those people did not take kindly to competition or loss of their product. At least this was quite a bit that would not ever hit the streets.

Anya still had not decided which side Philip was on. He and Joel seemed to have some sort of agreement, and he always seemed to be helping in the right places and the right way, but he sure hung out with iffy characters sometimes. Not even counting all the times he had been shot.

Anya asked the Harbor Master if she could move her houseboat closer to the tethered end of the dock. She didn't want to be so far out away from land right now. He told her she could move it right up next to the steps, if she wanted, as that berth was not reserved at present. It would be noisier during fishing season when all the boats were occupied and crews were coming and going at all hours of the day and night.

She might regret it later, but for the present, she really wanted to be closer to shore and possible help if she needed it. While they were talking about it, they decided why not just move her right now while she had help handy. She fired up the engine and the men cast off from the dock after unplugging the water and power connections.

The Harbor Master piloted the boat over to it's new mooring and they had her hooked back up and tied off in short order. Spike grumbled about the move, then settled back in on his perch on the roof so he could watch everything going on. Anya figured he would soon be getting treats from almost everyone using the steps and dock. She considered painting some signs asking folks to please not feed the guard raven.

Spike added growling to his repertory. She wasn't sure where he had heard growling, but he did it very well. He usually spoiled the growling by chortling when someone jumped.

Anya continued her two jobs all through winter. Her paintings were still keeping her busy the rest of the time. She found interesting pieces of driftwood to make frames and had most of her work ready for Sandy's shop.

Chapter 16

Sandy decided to have an art show, just for her work and maybe add a couple by other local folks if they were interested. She planned on advertising it in Juneau and a few other towns in the immediate area. Then word got around and several other folks wanted to show items they were making, so they decided to see about making it a community event and using the Community Center hall again.

Carmen informed the Mayor they should make it an annual event and help advertise the town to increase tourism. He thought he had a fine idea there and proceeded to make it an even larger event. A town BBQ of seafood, a book fair, the art show and boat races to make a week long festival out of it. They could think of other things to round out a full week of festivities now that he had set the ground for them. Anya didn't know how Carmen managed to smile and say "Yes, sir."

"Don't you ever feel like pouring itching powder down his shorts or something?"

Carmen busted up laughing and when she recovered, she said she got even in little ways but had not thought of the itching powder thing. By any chance, did Anya have any?

No, she had to get rid of hers after she doused George's underwear in it, and his entire underwear drawer after finding out he had a girlfriend.

His girlfriend was not enamored by his constant scratching and thought he had something contagious and broke up with him. He was in a foul mood for weeks after that and still scratching so she figured she better keep the bottle out of sight, burned it, then put it in the trash.

Sandy, Carmen and Anya put out a questionnaire around town and asked what everyone would like to see at the festival that they could manage to do. An idea box was placed in the entryway of City Hall and folks could drop off ideas any time.

Fishing Derby, ugly fish contest, best beard contest, log rolling contest, many ideas came in. They checked around to make sure they were not planning on a date that any of the neighboring towns held anything special and finally picked a date.

They picked almost all of the inexpensive contests that did not require a cash outlay to put on. Then they added the ones that people paid an entry fee to join and would pay for themselves to add. Finally, they tried to find a small carnival attraction of some sort that would agree to come on such short notice and were lucky enough to find a very small start up carnival that was trying to find bookings anywhere. Most were booked years in advance. The Mayor owned a barge that he made available to haul them north from Seattle.

Next, they had to find space for the carnival to put up their small attractions. The Mayor asked around and finally decided to just block off downtown and have it all set up on the streets as there was not enough level, open ground available anywhere. Almost everyone walked most of the time to get around town anyway, so it would not be much of a hardship to have to walk for a week. There would be plenty of advance notice for anyone needing to buy anything requiring a vehicle to haul away from the downtown area.

The Community Center was available at any time so Sandy, Carmen and Anya started getting it set up weeks in advance so there would not be any last minute rush on the art exhibit. Anyone that was interested in exhibiting was invited to bring their exhibits early enough to be sure of setting them up to the best advantage for displays.

The local Native Arts Center was enthusiastic about exhibiting also, so was getting an impressive display ready from their many members. Since many were members of the

Raven Clan, they were certainly going to compliment Anya's exhibit, too.

The male population was looking pretty scruffy with the ongoing attempt to at least place somewhere in the beard contest. One lady, Louise, decided she could do a better job than her husband on growing a beard and went off her hormone pills for the duration. She was right. She was growing a luxuriant curly beard and was doing it in style, with small braids and ribbons laced through and curls added around the edges.

Then she started really styling it and made it into a daily topic around town, just guessing what she would do with it next. She was such a pretty woman no one expected something like this from her. She looked like a double for a young Ann Margaret (movie star, look her up).

Most of the island's residents were enthusiastic about the upcoming event, except a few of those 500 soreheads the sign in the harbor mentioned. It's not that the town was so civic minded or even patrons of the Arts. But by the end of winter, everyone was looking for something different to do and this certainly was something different for this small community.

There was always the family fights and breakups that accelerated in winter and the drinking that went on no matter what. In good times, they drank to celebrate and in hard times, they drank to drown their sorrows. Some people just never get past their Terrible Two's mentality.

Carmen was having fun with the whole Arts Festival thing and came up with several ideas that added a lot to the whole plan. It had grown beyond a simple art exhibition to a full scale town production. She wanted to call it "Break Out Of Winter" then decided to hold a contest to name it. Since it was going to be held in June, it was a little bit late for breaking out of winter, anyway.

Sandy was in a frenzy of advertising and getting the word out, everywhere she could manage for free. She sent out news releases by the ream and her internet provider should have given her a bulk rate discount. She figured she probably financed months of the operating budget for the postal service all by herself.

Anya was in a daze. She was glad people were enjoying her painting, but she never expected anything like this to happen because of it. Sandy even contacted Ruben Jones, the art buyer that had expected Anya to jump at the chance to be discovered. He was sending a couple of people North to report on the proceedings and interview Anya for national coverage. Sandy was excited about it, Anya wasn't so sure she wanted national coverage.

There would be another auction held at the end of the week long festivities and she was nervous about that.

Sandy wanted her to be present at the auction and help in the sale. She wasn't sure her nerves could handle the suspense. Would people still like her work enough to bid and buy it? Would she be a disappointment to them in person?

She painted in every spare moment she could find. Her days at the gift shop were spent painting, also. People dropped in all the time to see how she was doing and how Spike was. A few people had approached her about teaching some classes in painting. She wasn't sure about being able to teach, she was mostly self taught and no formal training to teach anyone else. After she talked it over with Sandy, she told everyone interested, if they wanted to come paint while she was painting, they were welcome.

Sandy ordered some painting supplies to stock and soon was selling as many supplies as actual artwork in the off season for tourists. She let Anya order wholesale through her suppliers so it saved a lot on expenses for her.

Anya was still making all her own frames for her artwork, which was time consuming. Philip stopped by one evening while she was working on the deck of her home, cutting driftwood pieces to use and asked if he could help. He told her woodworking was one thing he truly enjoyed doing.

He wanted to make a frame for one of her works that he really liked, so she let him do the whole thing. He did such a wonderful job on it, she agreed to let him make as many as he wanted and it would free up a lot of her time. He could work on her deck during the day, she had all her tools set up out in the screened in porch area.

Spike usually accompanied him while he beach combed for driftwood to use and they were becoming quite chummy. Spike did not like being left home when she went to work, so this worked out well for them all.

While they were searching a stretch of beach a bit farther from town than usual, Spike got interested in something over under a pile of drift and was squawking and pulling at something when Philip approached. Spike had scared the gulls off with his arrival and he finally pulled something loose from whatever he was picking at. He flew back to Philip with it and dropped a bright shiny key into Philip's hand.

Philip continued over to the pile of drift and then almost wished he had continued on past without investigating. The battered body of one of the fishermen he had seen in town was under the pile of drift and it didn't look like he had been there very long. When he checked, he actually found a heartbeat. The man didn't look like he should still be alive, but Philip was going to try to make sure he stayed that way.

He rushed back to the nearest phone and called Joel and told him the what and where, and went right back to try to give any assistance possible to the injured man. He uncovered the man and checked for broken bones. One leg was possibly broken or dislocated and one shoulder was dislocated, also. Philip knew there was no doctor available and it would take hours to get one over from the nearest town that had one. So he straightened, then slowly pulled the bones into alignment. The shoulder audibly popped back into place, the leg took a bit more adjusting to get the bones all aligned correctly.

When the rescue team arrived, they put splints on the leg and taped the shoulder to his body to hold him for the trip through the surf to the waiting boat that would take him to the closest town with a hospital and doctor. The leader of the rescue team told Philip he did a great job on both the shoulder and the leg and he would let him know how the fellow did.

Philip carried his load of driftwood to Anya's boat and stored it on the boat deck to dry. He remembered the key that Spike had given him when finding the injured man.

It looked like a locker key. He walked over to the jail to talk it over with Joel. Joel thought maybe it was to a locker at the airport, since those were the only ones in town, so they drove across the island to the airport on the other side.

They found the locker and opened it carefully. Inside was a digital camera and a small tablet. They carefully removed both, wearing gloves and placed them in a plastic bag. Philip suddenly felt the small hairs on the back of his neck raise and murmured to Joel that he thought they were being watched.

Joel said he felt it too, but thought he was overreacting. They both figured they better be very careful or they could end up like the fellow just rescued or worse.

They walked over to the ticket counter and asked about tickets to Juneau leaving as soon as possible and told there was a flight scheduled to arrive in 5 minutes and leave in 15, if they cared to go that soon. They did.

It was just a small commuter flight, but they weren't picky. They called Juneau just before time to leave and asked to be met at the airport on arrival.

The flight was quick, uneventful and very bumpy. The Trooper that met the flight was glad to escort them back to headquarters. Someone found a connection that would fit the camera and they downloaded the contents to a laptop to check before placing it directly into the system computers in case it was some bug or virus.

Instead, it was a series of photos of some labs being set up in the forests on islands around Southeastern. There were dates on the pictures and corresponding information in the little booklet. The booklet named names of local people involved. There were not many truly local people but quite a few of the seasonal residents with boats were named. A couple of politicians were included. The book was a treasure house of information and the photos backed the information. Its easy to say someone's notes or memory is mistaken. It is harder to dispute photos of the incidents taking place.

A list of names was drawn up to have warrants sworn out and taken to a Judge for his signature. This was going to shake loose a lot of worms in the system.

By the time Joel and Philip made it back home, they were totally worn out and too tired to notice being followed from the airport to town. On the curve overlooking the ocean before reaching town limits, an old car started to pass then swerved into the side of Joel's pickup. His reflexes still were good enough to keep them from going over, but just barely. That woke them both up. They proceeded more cautiously and made it into town.

"So, someone WAS watching us, earlier. I'm really glad to have that stuff in Juneau instead of trying to keep it secure here until we could get someone to either come get it or mail it in."

"Yes, but good sports that they are, they couldn't resist trying to take us out anyway, even after we no longer have the evidence."

"Be careful, they don't take kindly to being thwarted."

Chapter 17

The fishing boats were all in harbor for the spring openings and would stay through the summer and fall, usually, so all the spaces were filled in the small harbor.

Anya usually liked having her houseboat closer to the stairs, but late at night after a crew got paid, it was sometimes a noisy place to live. Tonight was not one of the nights she enjoyed living in this location.

One of the new boats in harbor had a large crew for so small a boat and they were extremely ill mannered. Sandy convinced her to purchase a 12 gauge shotgun and helped her reload some birdshot shells with rock salt. She had one rock salt shell, then a birdshot shell in the magazine, then a slug. If she got to the slug, she wanted them permanently down.

She found a very nice informative book on wild edible plants and purchased it. She also found a better backpack than the one she had used from the can dump. After her experiences then, she kept the backpack filled and ready to go at any time, just in case. She did not want to think she was a paranoid person, but she did not always feel very safe now.

She kept her pack locked in a cabinet on deck, so if she needed it, she would not even have to come inside to get it. She was afraid she had over packed it and might have to empty some out, if she had to go very far, packing it, but maybe she could cache items then and retrieve them later. She just knew she did not want to feel helpless again as she had when she first woke up tied to that bed.

The painting classes were going very well. She did not teach, but she showed how she painted and helped others that wanted to try it. Sandy told her that is what the best teachers did, show how instead of just lecturing.

As the festival drew closer, it took on a life of it's own. Just when Anya thought she could not possibly manage anything else, someone seemed to always have an answer or lend a helping hand.

Sandy was at her best and thrived on taking care of details. She had her group of friends all handling the different sections of town that were each doing something different and the assorted contests.

It looked like Louise was going to win the beard contest or at least the most decorative beard section, hands down. Everyone was betting on her.

They had built a special shallow pond for the log rolling contest and several people, both men and women, were practicing. Someone set up a greased pole to try walking. It was not very far off the ground, but it was still difficult.

The small carnival was reported as loaded onto the barge and headed North. Everyone in town was excited to see how it was going to be set up. Even the soreheads were starting to lend a hand here and there. They still didn't think it was going to be successful, but at least it was more interesting than anything else happening around the area. Carmen convinced one of the more vocal ones to show off his juggling skills while walking around town and he was very good at it.

He drew the kids like a magnet and always had a trail of kids following along behind him. Soon he was showing them how to juggle and lots of small jugglers were now wandering around town, trying to juggle everything they found along the way.

The day the barge landed and the carnival started unloading, it might as well have been declared a holiday as everyone stopped whatever they were doing and went to watch. Even though the area set aside for them to set up seemed large before they got there, after they started unloading, it looked much too small.

All the equipment had been removed from the playground and the streets surrounding it closed to traffic so all the surfaces could be used for booths and whatever else had arrived.

There were a couple of small rides and an arcade, then several booths to test assorted skills. As carnivals go, it was very small and insignificant., but it was the first ever to come to their town and everyone was happy to see it there.

The art exhibits were all in place, and everyone was looking forward to seeing it all together, even though more than half the town probably had wandered through and helped out whenever needed, setting it all up.

Spike was not amused by all the hubbub and stayed on the boat most of the time. Anya was not sure she was too pleased with it all, either and kept him company a lot of the time. Then she set up an easel behind the counter and lost focus on anything but painting and it was endurable.

As the night of the auction approached, Anya was back to being nervous again. She still wasn't secure in her painting enough to ignore any small suggestions that it wasn't good enough. She was almost wishing she was back in the little shelter she had improved in the ravine. Without the worry about food, water and TP of course. Especially without the worry that someone wanted to kill her. Other than that, the cave sounded pretty good.

After all her worrying, the actual auction was turning out to be a lot of fun. She didn't have to be up front in the spotlight so could watch from the back and bid on a few items she wanted from other people's work.

As the evening was winding down and her art was a great success, she began feeling like someone was watching her and not in a good way. She had not given in on leaving her gun at home, so did feel a bit more secure that she might be able to defend herself if needed, but did not want to have to.

She found Joel and Philip near the table set up for paying for the auction items and told them she didn't want to seem paranoid, but she was feeling something was wrong here. The men did not laugh away her fears, they took her seriously and for the first time since the feeling started, she felt like maybe they could control it.

Both men started paying closer attention to the people milling around in the Hall and anyone paying too much attention to Anya. It did not take them long to spot 2 men that were not obviously together, but that were never letting her out of their sight. They were inching their way through the crowd toward her at all times, slowly closing in. No one else noticed them and they were patiently waiting to get past several elderly people that were chatting in a group, heading for the exit.

Anya considered slipping out the rear entrance, until Philip mentioned there may be more waiting out back as these seemed to be edging her toward the back of the Hall. That scared her into staying inside.

When a child screamed when one of the men stepped on it's fingers, Anya used the diversion to slip under the table covering on the table the men were guarding with the money from tonight's auction and sale. She was completely hidden from view all the way around and stayed sitting flat on the floor. She had been in more comfortable places, but at the moment, it was a refuge.

She could tell the moment the men knew they had lost sight of her. They started pushing their way through the crowd. There were enough people in the crowd that still prized good manners to complain and complain loudly about the method of progress and soon someone threw a punch to enforce the complaint.

It had been a while since there had been a good rousing brawl in town and most folks seemed to join in cheerfully. The elderly, some women and children eased to the outside edges, some rooting for their own champion of the moment. The two instigators must have been used to crowds in the Lower 48 that all stood back and pulled out their phones to take pictures or video but would never think of joining in.

Louise, with her movie star good looks and flowing beard was working her way toward Joel and Philip, bashing heads with her purse as she strode through the crowd. Few knew she carried a large handgun in her purse and it made it a very firm club. When one of the strangers started to grab her, she clocked him firmly over the head and he went down for the count. The other one saw her hit his accomplice and started for her, only to have her husband clothesline him, then smack him.

Louise continued up to Joel and asked what they should do with them now that they had them? Joel figured he could hold them overnight on drunk and disorderly although there was no evidence of being drunk. The fight stopped just as quickly as it had started and Anya crawled out from under the table.

People were helping each other up and laughing. It had been a rousing good fight. Joel, Philip and Louise's husband, Dick, escorted the two strangers to the jail. A search before locking them up found no ID but some baggies of white powder and a gun, some knives and a straight razor.

Behind the Community Center they found

another ratty old van. Windows painted over on the inside and seats removed. Did these guys go buy these vans by the barge load? When the plates were called in, they were reported stolen in Washington State a few weeks ago but the vehicle did not match the plates.

The next day, they finally found a VIN number that had not been removed and called it in. The registration was for a wanted felon in Anchorage. The photo that followed was of one of their captives. This would be a third strike for him.

The other captive would not give his name but his fingerprints were in the system also and he was wanted in Washington State. They must have wanted him fairly badly as they started extradition paperwork immediately upon being notified of his location.

The Troopers from Anchorage were on the next flight down, so they wanted their man fairly badly also. Joel was happy to hand him over. Neither man would talk at all, so they had no idea why they were still after Anya.

Joel thought he ought to set up a camp for prisoners similar to the prototype in Arizona, in tents, wearing pink, doing public works to earn their keep. The cold, wet, conditions here should be a major deterrent if the colors and having to work were not enough. They never did have really great meals as Joel fixed them exactly what he fixed for himself and he was no cook. One prisoner had even offered to do the cooking while here. Joel was tempted.

When Carmen tallied up the income from the festival, she said the town had certainly raised enough money to put in the park they were always wanting, near the harbor. Anya suggested they ask for volunteer labor while the boat crews were mostly still in town and see if they could get it built even cheaper. Make a picnic workday of it and supply a buffet lunch for all helpers. Then whatever was left to do, use the money. Carmen was going to suggest it to the Mayor so he could make it his idea and get it passed by the Council.

Chapter 18

Anya decided while the weather was fairly good and nothing much happening at the moment, to go ahead and spend a few days up at "her" cave. She mentioned it to Philip and he saw no reason why she shouldn't, if that was what she wanted to do. She wanted to pick some berries while there, to bring back for winter and also take a sketch pad.

She arranged for some time off at the store and from the gift shop, also. Sandy would miss her setting up and painting when the large tour ships were in dock, but none were scheduled for the next couple of weeks.

While finalizing everything she wanted to take in her pack, that evening, she overheard some men talking, farther down the dock near one of the "outsider" fishing boats. She was working quietly, back under the overhang on her deck and no lights on, so the men were not aware she was listening.

She never tried to listen in on the conversations, but sound carries very well over water and she started listening when she heard her name mentioned. Then some laughter that she did not like the sound of and then more low conversation.

She decided to leave right now. She locked the door and loaded on her pack and started up the steps to the upper dock. She heard steps on the dock behind her and speeded up her walk just a little so she was on dry ground and ducked in behind a dry docked hull that was used as a sign for the harbor.

She stretched out flat on the ground and snuggled in under the hull a bit and was in deep shadow. It was not really dark and she could see the group of men that got onto her boat. One knocked on her door as the others stepped around out of sight of anyone inside.

Her lock was not a state of the art lock and the fellow soon had her door standing wide open. She made a mental note to see to that when she returned. The rest of the men went in and sounds from inside her home let her know they were doing a complete search for her and not being too careful about it, either.

Someone noticed from one of the other boats and the alarm was raised. While the melee was going on, on her boat, she scooted out from under the hull and started away from the docks. Spike was on his way home when he saw her and landed near her to see what was happening. She kept walking and he soon flew on ahead to the trees near the edge of the road. This was the site of the proposed future park for the town. She headed deep into the woods and soon found a protected area she could use for a camp tonight. She did not want to stumble around in the woods farther out in the dark and hurt herself.

Spike grumbled about not being in his comfy chair. That bird was spoiled, but she had brought a sweater he liked to sit on, so he finally settled in on it. She thought it was probably dangerous for a bird to sleep on the ground, but wasn't sure what she could do about it. Maybe her presence would deter any predator from attacking Spike during the night.

It was his low growl that woke her up the following morning. She quickly repacked her pack and they were on the move within minutes. She was willing to trust Spike's instincts on what might be dangerous when she could not see anything at all.

They continued hiking, sticking to the higher ground instead of the easier walking along the beaches or road. She stopped after a couple of miles and fixed them both some breakfast. All the freeze dried foods and dehydrated that she had bought during the winter was certainly lighter to pack and added variety to her meals that she appreciated. She had still included a large bag of rice.

When she finally arrived at the shelter, she

felt almost like she had returned home. She stored her supplies inside and started picking up firewood to add to the pile left inside. She had some camo bug net and put it across the opening to make it easier sleeping inside at night. She was not sure whether Spike would want to be inside or not as he usually preferred outdoors.

She showed him how to scoot under the edge of the net and he soon was going in and out like a pro.

Things were not exactly like she left them, in her shelter and she wondered if Philip may have used it during some of the times he was not around town. Everything was restocked, but several candy bars were added to the items in jars in the food cache.

Her small water hole was lined with rocks now, also, to keep the sides from caving in easily. There was a dipper cup hanging in a bush beside the little water hole. Small thoughtful things to make it a much nicer place to live for a while.

Anya filled all her water containers and placed them on a rock shelf in the back of her shelter. She carried a few more flat rocks in to place around in the shelter to have as shelves or seating. She built a better fire pit while she was at it. She had a small piece of sheet metal in her pack and she placed that over the rocks for a cook surface.

Each day when she was picking berries, if she found a cedar tree, she cut a few small branches to place in her shelter for the lovely odor. She figured it helped keep insects away, also. A few twigs of it added to her fire while cooking made a most wonderful odor in the shelter for a long time after she was done.

Most of the berries were not ripe yet, it was still too early in the summer for the best picking. But she enjoyed hiking around looking for the few in sheltered areas.

When she awoke, the rain was pouring down and dripping over her entrance. The net helped keep most of it out of the shelter and she was glad she and Spike were both inside. Summer storms usually didn't last very long and she hoped this was a very short one. She had a couple of books in her pack to read and her small sketch book, so she sat near the entry and did a series of rainy day sketches.

By the end of the second day of rain, she was more than ready for it to quit. By the third day, she started to worry a little bit. There was a fairly good sized stream running down the ravine. There was still quite a ways to go before it threatened to come into her shelter, but that could change in a hurry if the storm increased.

By the fourth morning, the rain had slacked off a lot and it was more wind than rain. She stayed indoors as much as possible so there would not be footprints in the soft dirt around her shelter. There were enough flat stones around to step on them going and coming to the shelter if she were careful.

It didn't take many days for the running water to stop and the ravine dried out fairly well. She was already a little bit overdue back in town, although she had not given any specific date for her return. She was pretty sure she had been out here close to 3 weeks now. The berries were ripening very well and she had quite a supply drying and dried to take home with her when she did go.

Salmonberries, under ripe highbush cranberries and huckleberries would add to her diet this coming winter. She did not like the highbush cranberries once they were fully ripe, but the half ripe ones were quite good.

One morning about the time she decided she probably should go back to town and see what had happened to her boat, she heard something coming up the trail in the ravine. She ducked into the bushes near the entrance to her shelter and sat very still. Spike was up in a tree nearby and was staying very quiet. Then he started chortling and flew down to meet the person walking up the trail.

Anya waited until she was sure of the identity of the person before she stood up and Philip jumped when she seemed to appear from nowhere. Spike landed near them and chortled happily. Philip tossed him the remains of the piece of jerky he was chewing on.

They sat on some old stumps in the sunshine and he asked how she was doing. He missed seeing her around town.

Anya told him she was fine and wondered how her boat had fared after the men broke into it the night she left.

He told her he and Joel ended up getting there shortly after the other crews had pretty much captured the ones on her boat. They were all booked on disorderly conduct until they could get reports back on fingerprints taken from the whole crew.

A couple of them had tried escaping by jumping overboard and trying to swim away, but a small enclosed boat harbor offers very little in the way of escape. With all the other boats turning on their search lights and the half dusk of a summer Southeastern Alaskan night, there was no hiding.

No one knew where she was, so everyone accused the vandals of somehow doing away with her. There was talk of lynching them which no one tried to keep quiet and some of them were confessing to other crimes to get out of being accused of this one. Drugs seemed to be the one thing they all had in common. Someone was planning on large scale drug manufacturing in the area somehow.

As she turned to go into her shelter, her shirt caught on a stick and pulled away from the waist of her jeans. Philip saw what looked like a large bruised area in the small of her back and asked her if she was okay.

She said sure she was, why?

He asked about the large bruise on her back and she told him she didn't have a bruise, but when she was escaping from the burning shack, she had somehow scraped her back and it was sore for quite a while after, but felt okay now.

Philip pulled out his digital camera and asked if he could take a picture so she could see what her back looked like? She said sure and turned her back., pulling her shirt up a little bit and holding it so he could take his picture. He was silent for so long, she started to wonder just what he was doing and turned around.

"Anya, you have a tattoo on your back."

"No,. I don't. I have never wanted or gotten any sort of body art."

He showed her the screen on his camera and she could see some sort of dark markings across the middle of her back. It looked almost like a list but was too small to make out exactly what it was. He asked if he could take more pictures to have it all on his camera so he could enlarge it on his laptop and see just what was on her back.

She wriggled her jeans down a little bit and he said that was all that was needed, the tattoo seemed to end just at her waist. He turned her into the light and took several shots of the tattoo so he would be sure of getting ones he could see very well.

Anya was royally upset. If George was not already dead, she would have made him wish he were. How dare he knock her out and then make her a target for every drug lord wannabe in the State? And a tattoo?

He knew she did not want body art, that was his thing but she just didn't want it on herself although she liked some of the ones he did on himself and friends. He was actually quite good at it. But this was not even art. Some sort of list, sheesh.

How could she get something that big removed? It was ugly and not even in pretty colors.

She was still steaming as she packed her gear to head back to town. Philip helped her close down her camp so it would remain unnoticed by anyone yet be partially stocked if needed in the future. He confirmed he had used it a while when he left her boat after that last crease in his side was almost healed.

They hiked at a fairly good pace with him carrying the larger load and then they skirted around town a bit to come in behind the gift shop and Sandy's place.

Sandy about strangled her, hugging her when they came in the back door. Once she got loose, she asked Sandy to look at her back and pulled her shirt up and pants lower. Sandy first thought it was a bruise, also, until she got closer and could read it. Philip asked if he could look at the photos on her computer from his camera so he could enlarge them and read it better.

They went into her office and set it up then each tried making sense of the lists. Philip emailed them to Joel's office with copies to the State Troopers and himself. He figured if they got the lists out and spread around, maybe that would take the pressure off and people would leave Anya alone. She certainly hoped so.

Chapter 19

The Trooper in charge of the drug task force in Alaska was on the next flight to talk to Anya and Philip.

He went over every detail of her ordeal from the walking in the door and George punching her to her current problems. He talked to Philip in a separate room, so she had no idea what they talked about. But they shook hands when they separated at the door.

A female Trooper accompanied him over from Juneau and Anya was asked if she would allow them to search her back for more information, just in case the one tattoo was not the only one. Sandy stayed with Anya and they went to Sandy's bedroom to look her over.

Sandy thought the small brown dot looked odd below the tattoo and when she touched it, Anya said that spot itched. The Trooper asked if she could touch it and after inspecting it, she said she thought it was something under the skin, it did not look quite right to be a birthmark or beauty spot.

They called the health aide and she came over with some supplies in a bag. After looking the spot over, she agreed, it appeared to be something just under the skin. Anya asked if she could remove it, please.

They took several pictures, then video of the removal of the spot and it was indeed something under the skin. They placed it in an evidence bag and followed procedure to safeguard it as uncontaminated evidence. The camera was included in another evidence bag.

Philip let her know he had to accompany the Troopers back to Juneau, but everything was okay and he should be seeing her in a few days.

Joel came over and they talked a bit before the Troopers left. Joel and Sandy would take her back to her boat and help her check it out.

Spike was waiting on a piling as they walked down the stairs to the floating dock. Outwardly, her boat looked fine. Inside was a different story.

When her home was searched, they didn't even try to be careful of her possessions. Tubes of paint were smashed on the floor, canvases slashed and books torn. Her clothes were ripped and slashed and across the mirror was a message, "We want your back."

She would have thought they had very bad grammar and not known what they were talking about if Philip had not seen her back.

Joel suggested she stay at Sandy's, if it was okay with Sandy. Sandy told her to just move back into the apartment, it was empty at the moment. They could even bring Spike's chair back. She kinda missed having them around.

Anya finally gave up trying to find any clothes she could wear. Everything was damaged in one way or another. She finally got some large trash bags and started bagging up the clothes to take to the dump. Sandy helped her in her bedroom and Joel started picking up the mess in the living room and kitchen.

One of the captains farther down the dock came over to see what was going on and when he looked inside, he whistled and asked what he could do to help. Joel asked if he could check out the engine and make sure it was not sabotaged in some way. He said his crew were much better at that then he was and he would be right back. Soon others showed up to help and they worked all afternoon fixing all they could on her boat.

Somehow they had left her planters alone and someone along the dock was watering them while she was gone, so they were full of produce. It was the only bright spot in her whole afternoon, other than the nice neighbors helping out.

Joel was telling them about the Troopers taking photos and evidence from Anya's back and it was all in Juneau, now. He figured maybe everyone wanting the evidence would now leave her alone if they knew the

Troopers already had it. Word would spread fast along the dock. When he stopped in on his rounds later, at one of the bars, he heard about it from one of the bar flies that never left his stool at the bar as long as the bar was open. Word travels fast in a small community.

Anya went back to work at the store and also continued working the rest of the week at Sandy's gift shop. Sandy was considering expanding into the empty rooms next to her shop. She owned the whole building, but just never got around to expanding it before. Now she liked having the art work and paint supplies, so wanted to enlarge the area they would occupy.

Most of the canvases ruined on the boat were empty canvases, but all of Anya's painting supplies were ruined and several of the canvases just had sketches on them and were ruined also. She tried resketching most of the ones that she could tell what had been ruined. Others were a total lost cause. At least all the finished and partly finished work was at the gift shop.

Sandy let her reorder paints and canvases wholesale through her contacts. That was a big help in getting restocked. She did keep paints at the shop also, but most had been ruined on her boat and now made her floor a rainbow of splashes and globs.

Her furniture, such as it was, would all need

replaced, also. She wanted to redecorate but at her own pace, not like this.

Sandy led her to a spare room in the unoccupied section of the large building. It was jammed full of assorted furniture. Sandy told her to pick out what she could use or liked. It was all used furniture, but in pretty good shape until she could get whatever she really liked to replace it whenever she wanted to.

The furniture was in excellent shape and beautiful. Anya looked at Sandy with hundreds of questions in her eyes, but not sure how to ask any of them.

Sandy laughed, but not a happy laugh. "My ex-husband. The lying SOB left me to pay the bills for all his fancy furniture he liked to have around him. After he left, I couldn't stand to look at it and almost had a very expensive bonfire out back. Then I figured maybe someday, someone could use it, so here it is. You can help yourself. It is all paid for, finally. Keep it or burn it, I will never use it."

Anya picked out a few items to replace the ones trashed on her boat and when Joel stopped by, checking on them later, he offered to move them for her after he got off shift.

He brought a couple of friends and they loaded and unloaded the furniture as though it were easy. The stairs were a bit steep as the tide was out, but they managed it fine. They removed the damaged furniture and would drop it off at the dump when they left.

Sandy came over as they were leaving and said the stuff looked so much better in Anya's home than they ever looked in hers. Anya thought it gave her home quite a bit of class and hoped she could do it justice. She didn't want to be snoopy, but wondered just how any man could leave such a wonderful woman as Sandy.

Sandy told her he just disappeared one day and no idea how or where he went. They had been arguing so much about his habits and even though he was an adult and capable of making his own decisions, he expected her to bail him out every time he made wrong ones. He told her some people he owed wanted their money right now and she told him he better find a job and pay them then. He got mad and stormed out. She had not seen him since.

Anya wondered if Sandy was as uncaring as she sounded about her husband leaving. Then she thought how she had been feeling about the way George had been treating her. He would push her and shove her until she fell, technically not hitting her until that last night, but still knocking her down. He did work once in a while, but not often and usually spent what he did earn on booze or drugs, so she didn't have many kind thoughts for him either.

Then Sandy started crying and said no matter what, once in a while she still missed the no good jerk. Anya knew that feeling, also. She figured they were very close to getting a divorce, but she sort of missed him now and then, when she remembered some of the good times when they first got married. She didn't hate him and certainly never wished for him to end like he did.

They sat for a while in the deepening dusk, then decided to fix a large salad and share it. Anya picked assorted greens from her planters and prepared a lovely salad and added some shrimp she thawed from her small freezer. They tossed some shrimp to Spike on the deck while they ate. He appeared to be happy to be back on his comfy chair. He chortled and yipped a couple of times, then nestled in.

Joel stopped back by as they were putting dinner dishes away, and asked Sandy if she would like a ride home and then asked Anya if she thought she would be okay for the night, on the boat?

Until he mentioned it, she had not given it any thought and now it spooked her a little bit. Would she be able to sleep or would she be jumping awake at every creak and groan of the boat and dock shifting on the tide and the people using the stairs and dock? She didn't know, but was determined to find out.

A couple of hours after Joel and Sandy left, Anya was still sitting on the deck with her shotgun near her hands. She heard a set of footsteps approaching the stairs and start down them. She tensed as they drew nearer her boat, then passed on by to one of her neighbors boats.

After the third set of footsteps passed on by, she was positive she would never get any sleep at this rate and certainly none if she went inside where she would feel more confined and less in control.

She pulled out her backpack and unrolled her sleeping bag back in under the overhang on the deck where the deepest shadows were on her deck. No one could see her unless they were looking for her with a flashlight.

She pulled the shotgun in with her and promptly fell asleep. She awoke disoriented for a few seconds, as the underside of the deck roof was not her usual view in the morning. She held still until she got her bearings and then slowly slid out of her sleeping bag, sliding the shotgun with her.

She found one of the crew members from one of the fishing boats, asleep on the dock near her catwalk and went "Pssst, you want some coffee?"

He jerked awake and looked sheepishly at

her. "Yes, ma'am, I sure would. That dock is not so comfortable but somehow I managed to sleep through my shift. I am so sorry, ma'am."

"Your shift? What do you mean?"

He shuffled around a bit, then admitted all the boat crews were taking turns making sure no one bothered her any more. He was going to catch it for sleeping on his shift.

She asked who was going to tell them, anyway? She wasn't and she would get some coffee and breakfast going for them both.

He sat on the deck and she went inside. She made the coffee and they shared it while she made some pancakes for both of them and Spike. She didn't think they were all that good for the bird, but he loved them, so she always made him a couple.

The young fisherman enjoyed his breakfast then offered to do the dishes. She shooed him back to his boat and cleaned up after their breakfast. While putting the dishes away, she heard a light tapping at her door but no barking from Spike.

When she checked at the window, it was Philip. She was glad to see him and opened the door. He came on in and they sat down in the kitchen area after she poured him some coffee and herself another cup of tea. Then she told him she made the coffee for her night watchman and told him what the young man had said. He said that was not a bad idea and he was glad they were looking out for her.

She asked him about Juneau and he was evasive on details, just told her everything was okay, not to worry. She hated hearing that, it seemed that some of her worst times happened immediately after being told not to worry.

Chapter 20

Philip spent the night in his sleeping bag on her deck, under the eaves. She slept soundly for the first time in quite a while. She awoke to Spike yapping and barking, banging around on her deck and the sound of glass shattering in her front door.

She grabbed her shotgun, put plugs in her ears and eased her door open just in time to see someone wearing a facemask come bursting through her door. She pulled the trigger on the shotgun and blew him back out through the door and sudden silence sounded almost deafening.

Shouts were heard farther down the dock as the noise had roused others from their boats. She had trouble hearing anything from the blast of the gun in the enclosed area. The ear plugs helped, but her ears still rang.

She still had shells in her shotgun, but hurriedly loaded another in to replace the one used.

She edged to the shattered door and could see the one she had shot on her deck and no sign of anyone else on board. She slowly stepped out onto her deck and looked around, her shotgun at the ready. As she stepped out from under the overhang, something hit her in the back of the head and she went down.

When she awoke, she had the sinking feeling she had already done this once before. She was tied to a bed with something over her eyes. This time, she was tied facedown and someone had raised her shirt to expose the tattoo on her back.

At least the bed didn't smell like an old stinky fish shack but that was not all that reassuring. The rag over her eyes made her think maybe they planned on letting her go after they checked out her tattoo for themselves, at least she hoped so. She didn't think she could get lucky enough to escape twice in the same manner.

She held very still and tried to figure out exactly what she was smelling and feeling. It almost smelled like a hospital.

She heard footsteps coming and relaxed, trying to appear still unconscious. It sounded like two people came into the room. One asked the other why they bothered taking her, since they knew the police now had all the information and whatever was on the chip they recovered from her back. Without the chip, the information would probably be useless.

The other one thought maybe they could

figure it all out just from the tattoo. Maybe she knew more than anyone thought she did and could just tell them.

"No, I don't think she knows anything. As I hear it, she didn't even know George worked for us or had tattooed her until very recently. He knocked her out to tattoo her, even."

"How did you hear all of that?"

"I read the police report while I was in police headquarters. They were quite pleased to let me see it."

Who was this guy? The voice did sound a little bit familiar, but not as though she knew him, maybe had heard him on the radio or something.

"Yeah, well, once they decipher the tattoo and read it all, you won't be so welcome on that side of the counter at police head-quarters."

"It's about time I retire and head to Mexico or Belize anyway. Maybe even South America. I like some of the countries down there a lot and have enough now to enjoy life down there."

"Ha, once they know you are no longer in the trade, they will just kidnap you and steal your money. They won't have any use for a retired Legislator."

"Hush, she will be coming around soon and no need for her to know who we are. We can just turn her loose tonight after dark and let her wander around until someone finds her. She don't have a clue who we are or where she is, so it is safe."

The other one mumbled something she didn't hear as they walked back out the door. Somehow, she did not think the other man intended on her leaving here alive.

Her arms were getting cramped from being held in the same position for so long and she could not manage to get the bindings any looser. She wasn't sure, but thought she was held with zip strips. She had managed to move her head back and forth enough to loosen the rag across her eyes a small amount. She did not want to get it off as that would give the one man a reason if he needed one, to make sure she did not leave here alive.

She kept bending her wrists back and forth, trying to weaken the plastic strips if that is what they were. Her legs did not feel like they were restrained.

She heard footsteps again in the hall so held still again. Someone walked very close to her on the bed and whispered not to move, he was going to release her hands but leave the rag over her eyes, he would lead her out, but she had to follow and not try to see anything around her or especially not him.

She nodded her head and he cut the ties, then assisted her off the bed. He held her arm lightly and led her to the doorway. He

checked down the hall and then they hurried
out and down the hall toward an exterior
door.

They were almost to the door when another
door opened behind them and someone
stepped out and yelled "Hey".

He pushed her roughly out the door and
then they were running down a street. She
did not even know what town they were in.
She tried to lift at least the edge of her eye
covering and the man hissed, "Leave it alone,
let me get you away from here a bit, then you
can lift it, after I am out of sight."

They continued running and then she could
hear the water and it sounded like they were
now running along a dock. He pushed her
onto a boat and told her to lay down and
cover up and hold still, no matter what. Then
he left, running on down the street.

She removed the eye covering and huddled
under the life boat with an old tarp over her.
She could hear sounds of pursuit, then a
small amount of searching among the boats
and then the steps moved farther off down
the street.

Soon, she heard people getting on the boat
she was on and she held very still. The boat
cast off and soon was underway, heading out
to sea.

She overheard the captain talking to a crew
member near the lifeboat she was under and

he was complaining about the search underway for her. He told his crewman he thought they should just dock at one of the little towns instead of going back to Juneau. Too much going on there to suit him.

She could not tell if he would be in favor of finding her on his boat or just throw her over to keep from being hassled for harboring her. She decided to just stay put.

When they finally docked late that evening, she thought she recognized the sound of Spike, barking on the piling near the entrance to the harbor. Then one of the crewmen laughed about the mixed up raven and she knew she was almost home.

After they were docked and the sounds of the crew faded away, she carefully moved out from under the lifeboat. Looking around carefully, she did not see anyone nearby, so stepped over onto the dock.

She stopped briefly to look at her houseboat but it had crime scene tape around it and she did not feel like dealing with that, tonight. She made her way to the jail and walked in. Joel was dozing in a chair by his desk and he almost fell out of it when she said "Hi, Joel."

He helped her remove the remains of the plastic zip strips she had been restrained with and sat her down in his chair. She asked for water and the bathroom and he showed her where the bathroom was while he got her some bottled water from his fridge. He started some water heating on the hotplate he had in the office, also and made some instant soup to go with her water. He apologized for the stale crackers he had to go with the soup and she ate them anyway, saying they were delicious. He offered her another cup of instant soup, but she figured she better go slow or she might get sick.

He asked if he could call Philip to let him know she was okay and here, as he was still recovering from the blow to the head he received the morning she was kidnapped. His stitches were driving him crazy and he was worried about her, berating himself for losing her on his watch.

She said okay and he placed the call. Philip showed up in less than 10 minutes. Other than the goose egg on her head from being hit, she was in fairly good shape, only dehydrated a bit from her day on the ocean with no water. Joel finally placed several bottles of water beside her and she continued to drink them as they talked.

She told them about the man that seemed familiar and she thought was a Legislator. They looked at each other and nodded. That matched some of the information they had retrieved from the chip and her tattoo.

They let her sleep in the jail, with her

shotgun retrieved from the locker and her door unlocked. She figured jail was safer than home at present. She thought she would have trouble falling asleep and was surprised to find she slept soundly all night.

When she woke up, the sun was shining and she could hear voices in the main room down the hall from her cell. She had not undressed to sleep so smoothed back her hair and braided it a bit to get it under control before stepping out into the hallway with her shotgun.

She stayed out of sight and listened at the partially open door a while. Then she heard a commotion and someone running her direction. She stepped back and raised the shotgun just a little bit, so when the man burst through the doorway, she was far enough back and the gun was aimed at his middle, he stopped immediately.

Joel and a Trooper she did not recognize were right behind him and they grabbed the man from behind. He had somehow known she was back there and was intending on taking her hostage. He had not considered that she would be armed and not in a cell, locked up.

When they plunked him down in a chair, none too gently, she walked into the room, still holding her shotgun carefully pointed down, mostly, but still in his general direction.

There were several other Troopers and many prisoners, or she thought they were prisoners, crowded into the room.

They were trying to process and move them to the larger facilities in Juneau as fast as they could, but they had so many, it was taking longer than expected. They had pulled a raid in the very early morning hours and caught almost all of the people on the lists from her tattoo and chip.

The Federal drug enforcement people were running the show, but they used a lot of the local law enforcement people as they were familiar with the area and terrain. The large camp they found up the Stikine River was now completely captured with no loss of life to the officers and few injuries.

Due to the terrain and few communications available throughout Southeastern, they were holding raids against the other migrant camps they knew of from the lists. The conditions the workers were living in were appalling, the work they were doing was dangerous with no safeguards. Most of them surrendered thankfully, glad to be going back to the life they knew and conditions that may be terrible, but seldom as life threatening with no means of escape.

These camps were little more than forced labor camps. Once they were in one of the camps, they may be moved from camp to camp, but no one ever got to go home and there was no way to find out whether the money promised their families would actually be paid.

The Legislator Anya had heard, while a captive, was arrested while giving an anti-drug speech. He protested his innocence far and wide but the evidence told a different story.

While on vacation, he had been compromised, then promised no one would ever find out about it if he went along and developed the organization in Alaska. When the child's body was found, he caved in and once involved, expanded the operation beyond the wildest expectations of his South American handlers.

George seemed like a likely candidate for dumb labor setting up the camps and organization in Alaska, but was smarter than he acted. He gathered enough evidence and planned on turning them in, but got too confident of his invincibility. By the time he knew he was in trouble, he didn't see any way out for himself.

Anya was the only person close at hand the evening he knew they were out to get him, so he anesthetized her the fastest way he knew and tattooed the information on her back and inserted the microchip with all the locations and names just under the skin and tattooed a mole over it. He did not know they were closing in on him while he worked on her.

If he had not been so close to the booze bottle and tempted to try the product they were making, now and then, he probably could have managed what he intended without getting caught. But when he was drinking or high, he tended to brag about how smart he was and how much he knew. This should not have been one of those things to brag about.

As reports trickled in, Joel was kept busy as they coordinated the next island or camp to hit. An amazing amount of pot was found, considering the growing season wasn't the greatest for that, in this area. They must have just been using it as a possible side line and if it prospered, good, if it didn't, no biggy.

The labs set up were the main targets and they were being destroyed. The sheer volume of product confiscated was mind boggling. The amount of prisoners far exceeded the jail capacity of any jails available in Southeastern.

Joel decided to use some of the large tents they had confiscated from the migrant camps and set up tent city over on a small uninhabited island far enough out to discourage anyone from trying to swim for it. The island had been hit with a williwaw wind several years ago and then clear cut of all the downed trees, so there wasn't even materials to build a raft left on the island or anywhere to hide. The tents were set up on the level area cleared for a log landing when the island was logged and prisoners were boated over and dropped off. None of them were happy at this turn of events. They had all heard how good prisoners had it in American jails and most were looking forward to it.

Military surplus supplied large cooking containers to heat water for the whole camp. No steak and crab dinners at this camp. MREs would have to do it. The bosses were not allowed to go to the tent city camp. They were locked up but still got MRE's (Meals Ready to Eat) for their meals. No one was going to enjoy this time in jail. If MREs are good enough for our military, they are certainly good enough for criminals and illegal aliens.

Joel then put everyone to work, developing the tent prison into a neat organized camp. Latrines were dug and built over. Water storage was set up and shower houses built. No one had any idea how long the prisoners were going to be housed here, so it might as well be made as comfortable as possible. Military folding cots were flown in and set up in the tents, and foot lockers assigned to each inmate. Neon pink jump suits were handed out and as the weather started cooling down some, neon pink jackets. If pink was good for his hero in Arizona's jail, then it was good enough for Joel.

Soon heaters were set up in each tent and firewood details sent out to salvage slash from the logging. No axes were allowed, so larger pieces were not brought in but stacked for civilian crews to come over and cut to length, then the prison crews could bring them to camp. The island was going to be extremely neat by the time they left.

When they ran out of jobs to do, Joel managed to set up a tree planting program and thousands of seedlings were planted on the small island, starting at the top of the small hills on it.

Patrols combed the beaches, picking up trash and bagging it for removal. This island would be spotless when they were long gone.

Chapter 21

Anya finally felt like she could relax. No one should be out to get her now. Everything she possibly knew or had access to, was known to the Feds and State Troopers.

She and Sandy started cleaning up her boat, yet again. They removed the plywood that had been nailed over her broken door. The crime scene tape came down and she could sweep up her floor and try to find a door to replace the broken one.

As soon as word spread that she was back at the boat, several of the regular crew members from the boats around her came with offers of help. Even better, one man actually knew how to build a custom door to replace her broken one as it was not a standard sized door. He could still use the hinges from her door as they were made for use on salt water. He suggested a better type of door latch and lock system though, so she ordered that.

She would stay in Sandy's apartment until

the boat was ready to live on again. Spike was happy back on the upper deck dropping treats to the dogs below and barking at them.

Philip stopped by the apartment one evening while she was sketching a scene on a canvas. He told her this was his last job and he was retiring and looking for a different line of work. She suggested he talk to Joel as he was looking for someone to help him out. Small island police work was getting to be too much for one man to handle.

He said it was close to the old job, but shouldn't be as dangerous or hectic, anyway and he did have the training for it. He would talk to Joel tomorrow. Anya had finally figured out that Philip was one of the good guys. He was just undercover when she first met him.

She asked if he would miss the excitement of his old job and he said no, not a bit. The excitement was the worst part of the old job. He didn't know how a man could do that kind of job when he was worrying about the safety of the ones he loved at the same time.

She looked at him questioningly. Who was he worrying about? It couldn't be her, he only kissed her on the forehead like she was a 10 year old and not even that, lately.

She looked at him with those big gorgeous eyes and he just melted inside. She didn't have a clue. He slowly stood up and advanced to where she was on her sketching seat at her drafting table. He carefully placed a hand on each side of her without messing up her sketch and slowly lowered his face to hers.

The whisper soft breath she exhaled felt like angel kisses along his cheek. He carefully touched his lips to hers and softly, gently kissed her. She practically melted, right there. The next kiss was not as soft, but he never pushed her beyond what she wanted to experience at that moment.

He stepped back a bit and looked as shell shocked as she did.

"I love you, Anya, and would like to spend the rest of my life with you, if you don't mind."

Mind? Did she mind? She jumped up and threw her arms around his neck and practically leaped into his arms. The kiss she gave him should leave no doubt in his mind how she felt. But just in case, she did mention that she loved him also.

EPILOGUE

Sandy fussed with the veil over Anya's face and flicked a mosquito away. Then she adjusted the train down the back of the skirt. Finally Anya told her if she didn't quit fussing, she was going to change back into her camo pants and T shirt. The rain boots would be much more comfortable than these high heeled shoes.

Sandy finally stepped back, grumbling that the details made it perfect and she was going to have a perfect wedding if it disabled her. Those shoes were very fashionable and most women would have done anything to be getting married wearing a pair of them.

Anya heard the sounds of the music change and told Sandy she was on and as her Maid of Honor, she had to get going on time. Sandy grumbled some more but was smiling and headed for the door.

Joel stuck his head around the corner and asked if she was ready and he was going to walk her down the aisle as that was as close to a wedding as he hoped to ever get.

The music changed again and she took Joel's arm. They stepped out into the

Community Center as her little church didn't have enough room for all the people wanting to attend this special day for her.

Her Pastor was waiting at the end of the aisle and then she looked to his left and her breath caught. Philip was waiting for her. The look in his eyes was pure love. Her heart melted yet again and she only had eyes for him as Joel escorted her down the aisle.

When the Pastor asked who gives this woman, most of the town people stood up and said we do. Then they added he better be good to her or they would take care of it for her.

She had to laugh just a little bit at the stunned expression on Philips face. He whispered to her that he would never knowingly hurt her in any way. The Pastor cleared his throat and proceeded with the ceremony. She thought she heard Spike, chortling from the roof of the Hall ,when they were pronounced man and wife.